SOUTH OF THE ABYSS

Nebbid Werdna

Other Publications by the author:

Andrew Dibben's Norfolk Watercolour Landscapes, with Foreword by Dame Norma Major, was published to great acclaim by Halsgrove in 2002, and was reprinted a year later. (Currently out of print).

Andrew Dibben's Norfolk Waterscapes, a second volume from the same publisher, was published at the end of October 2005.

Boats, Beaches and Barns, a third, large format limited edition book, was self-published in 2010. (Out of print).

Working Boats and Heaths, a 44-page booklet, was produced to accompany the 2014 exhibition held in Holt.

The Girl From Burgundy, an account of the author's French family's origins and wartime experiences, was produced as a Limited Edition book in 2016.

Boats, Beaches & Barns of Norfolk and Suffolk, an extended version of the earlier title, with a Foreword by former Shadow Chancellor of the Exchequer Ed Balls, was published by Wall Road Publishing in 2017.
ISBN – 978-0-9956254-0-2

The Maritime Paintings of Andrew Dibben was published in February 2020 by Wall Road Publishing.
ISBN – 978-0-9956254-2-6

The Abyssworld - Drawings, Watercolours and Oil Paintings by Nebbid Werdna, was published by Wall Road Publishing in November 2020.   ISBN - 978-0-9956254-1-9

Andrew Dibben F.I.E.A., Dip.A.D.

Andrew Dibben became a full-time professional artist in 1989. He is primarily a watercolourist, noted for his highly detailed studio work, but has also worked extensively in the field, resulting in work of a looser appearance. He is known for his minutely observed paintings of small wooden boats, architectural subjects, and also expansive beach scenes.

Dibben has shown work regularly for some 30 years at The Gallery, Holt, in North Norfolk, and has had a number of one-man shows there, most recently in 2014 and 2019. He has also shown at Mandell's Gallery, Norwich, and various other galleries.

Andrew Dibben is one of the four founder members of the I.E.A. (Institute of East Anglian Artists), and is currently the Vice-President. See: www.eastanglianartists.com

Since 1977, he has shown work in many years with the Royal Institute of Painters in Watercolours (R.I.), the Royal Society of Marine Artists, the Society of Graphic Fine Art, and the Laing Competition.

In 2010, Dibben began working, on and off, on a side project of drawings and paintings of an imaginary world, entitled "Abyssworld". He adopted the pseudonym of *'Nebbid Werdna'* for this work, to separate it from his earlier works. This project has been taking up most of the artist's time recently. A book entitled **The Abyssworld** featuring the series was published to coincide with a major exhibition of the work staged at the Primeyarc Gallery in Great Yarmouth in late 2020/early 2021.

South of the Abyss is a work of fiction, written to complement the Abyssworld series of images. It has a slightly different emphasis, in that the action seems to be set on Earth rather than another world, but still features many of the fearsome geological obstacles of the picture series. Most of the illustrations in this book feature in *The Abyssworld*.

This edition: first publication 2021
Published by Wall Road Publishing, Gorleston, Great Yarmouth, 2021
wallroadpublishing@outlook.com

All characters and events in this publication are fictitious, and any resemblance to real persons, living or dead, is purely coincidental.

The moral right of Andrew Dibben to be identified as the author of this work has been asserted. Nebbid Werdna is a pseudonym of Andrew Dibben.

All images and text - copyright © Andrew Dibben 2021

Design, layout, and text by the author.

All rights reserved. No part of this publication may be reproduced, stored in a retrieval system, or transmitted in any form or by any means without the prior permission of the copyright holder.

ISBN - 978-0-9956254-4-0

Printed by Mixam UK, Watford.

The Formation of the Modern World

"It is believed that the Great Abyss was formed when a large meteorite hit the planet approximately 2,000 years ago. It struck a point at the junction between two tectonic plates, where the crust was particularly thin, plunging into a reservoir of molten magma. The impact set off a chain of cataclysmic events, resulting in the planet losing a portion of its surface water, as well as a certain amount of the atmosphere, both of which drifted off into space after being blasted into extreme altitude. Many large, coastal cities all around the world were totally destroyed by tsunamis which resulted from the collision. Understanding of the event was extremely sketchy at first, as news services were largely obliterated by it, but a few astronomers survived, and pieced together what had happened from the visible evidence. Conspiracy theories arose, claiming that there had been a nuclear strike and counter-strike by the world's super-powers, but these notions soon lost credibility when no radiation sickness ensued among the survivors. The event would later come to always be referred to as "*The Apocalypse*".

For many years, the atmosphere was obscured by debris and dust thrown up by the impact. Global temperatures were lowered by several degrees by this blanketing effect, counteracting the previous global warming trend. Countless numbers of species were driven into extinction by the deleterious effect which the sudden darker conditions had on the growth of plants and trees.

Despite all this, small pockets of humanity succeeded in surviving, particularly those positioned in areas already used to enduring long dark winters, in regions closer to the poles. These subsisted for a few years thanks to food supplies preserved in large commercial cold stores, as well as dried food produce. Hydro-electricity and nuclear power production persisted for a number of years, until failures were caused by the loss of maintenance knowledge within the community for the relevant technologies. But ingenuity resulted in the development of smaller-scale power production, and eventually in the reliable restoration of hydro-power and the large-scale development of solar and wind power, as well as geo-thermal energy.

Closer to the tropics and the equator, ash and dust had rained down on the surface for a period of years, burying arable land areas as well as cities in a thick layer which extinguished most life-forms. The planet's aspect changed completely.

But life on the planet had survived previous extinction events, and it survived this one too. Human life continued, albeit in tiny numbers, in far northern and far southern regions, despite near-impossible conditions, thanks to the application of remarkable innovations and sheer determination. Societies reformed slowly, and conditions on the planet gradually improved. Agriculture became possible once more, although marked by epic failures in some of the early years. Deciduous trees returned gradually, as carefully nurtured seedlings were raised in glass-houses, and could eventually be planted outdoors once more.

The early post-apocalypse small-scale societies were able for some years to make use of earlier technologies which had survived the impact event, making use of oil supplies held in large storage tanks. Oil production had ceased at the point of the impact however, and so, as supplies dwindled, a new source of power had needed to be developed quickly. Electric technologies won out; the impact-event survivors remembered the global warming which had resulted from the previous industrial revolution, and sought to avoid a repetition of this catastrophe.

The existence of electricity generation, and the survival of a small number of people knowledgeable in its production and useful application, ensured the survival of humanity. Without this technology, humans would have reverted to an existence resembling that which was current in the Earth's Dark Ages.

The meteorite strike resulted in the secondary effect of an electro-magnetic pulse, which was powerful enough to destroy the majority of portable electronic devices. Thus most means of communication were rendered inoperable following the cataclysm. This in turn meant that the small communities which survived the event found themselves totally isolated for a long period. It took courage and determination for people to reach out and make contact with other groups of survivors, and eventually reform communications networks and mutual support organisations.

A complex and extensive mechanised civilisation eventually returned over a period of three centuries; but its major centres were located much further north than previously. A few hardy pioneers gradually migrated slightly closer to the tropics, but water supplies were a constant problem. The planet had become much more arid, and weather patterns had altered radically."

Excerpt from the preface to *"A History of the Modern World"*
Michael Olinsson, Professor of Modern History, University of Laxberg
© Laxberg University Press, 1989PA

ONE

DANA

Dana was beside herself with worry now. She knew that she wasn't the only one in this situation, but she could no longer bear the waiting and worrying. She had made up her mind: she would make the long journey south to look for Garth.

It had been eight weeks since she had last heard from him. He had travelled down to the southern polar region to give technical support to a team attempting to restore a reliable power supply in the city of Mandela. There had been an unusually long and powerful meteorite storm that year, and there were even rumours that some strikes had occurred beyond the end of the normal season, and far to the south of the usual 'meteorite alley', the central band of largely desert terrain which girdled the world. This meant that, worryingly, Garth might conceivably have been in an area receiving a strike.

Aside from the extra-terrestrial hazards, there had been stories of political unrest in the southern regions, whose inhabitants always felt the poor relations, compared to those living in the wealthy north. None of this had reached the television news channels, but rumours circulated fast among the population, despite government suppression.

Telephone communications were completely disrupted, as often happened at this time of year. It was a combination of telecoms towers being struck by meteorites, and the above-average solar flare activity yielding high radiation levels. Phone calls within the city usually worked, albeit with a high degree of crackling and hissing, but longer-distance calls just resulted in 'number unobtainable' tones, or heavy white noise.

Officially, travel through the Central Belt was forbidden, because there was still the risk of an occasional strike by a smaller meteor, which could easily destroy a vehicle. The all-clear would only be given in another two to three weeks' time; but even then, the highways might not have been diverted around any new craters, so any journey faced long delays, with roads taking appallingly rough temporary routes around new obstacles. Even so, Dana knew of a number of people who had defied the odds, as well as the Government regulations, to travel during meteorite season. She wasn't going to let rules stop her. Yes, it was potentially dangerous, but she just couldn't bear the not knowing any longer...

She had begun to prepare for the trip a few days ago, with a two-week leave from work scheduled to begin in a couple of days' time. Dana worked as an Assistant Lecturer of History at the University of Laxberg. The Spring break was due anyway, but she thought that she would be able to plead for a slight extension of her leave, should it prove necessary.

The worst part had been when she went to tell her parents of her plan. She had not wanted to deceive them, so had explained everything in detail. Her mother had been horrified at the idea, and tried hard to dissuade her from making the trip. Although her father had made a show of supporting his wife's objections, Dana thought that she could detect in him a measure of pride and admiration in his daughter's adventuring spirit. He had always been a bit of a rebel in his younger days, and here she was, demonstrating the same traits.

She had bought food that would keep well, large containers of water, and extra fuel cells for the car. She had downloaded the entire latest version of the Encyclopedia to her tablet. She had studied maps to plan her route. The highways across the Central Belt were sparse, but some routes offered a better chance of finding a parallel alternative road in case of an obstruction. She would leave her green and forested homeland, and pass right through the big city of Laxberg, then head south-east towards the Great Abyss, crossing a number of rifts, before arriving in a civilised region once more. The trip would involve almost seven days' driving, which she thought about with a mixture of excitement and extreme trepidation. It was several years since she had last headed into the desert region, and the prospect of doing this alone was a little frightening.

She had told her neighbours that she was taking a break away, and most of them assumed she would be heading for the sea or the mountains, well to the north of 'Meteorite Alley'. Once south of the city, she didn't think that she would attract that much attention, despite the travel ban, because there were always service engineers on the road, going to fix problems. As long as she wasn't stopped by police, all would be fine. She had dungarees and a hard hat to give the right look, so felt reasonably confident in that respect, and her vehicle looked suitably utilitarian. She had decided to take Garth's four-door pickup truck for this journey; it was more rugged, and newer, than her small car.

Dana was still unable to contact Garth the evening before her departure. She would try phoning again in the morning, before setting out, but her intuition told her that she wouldn't reach him, and that something was wrong. She went to bed, but slept fitfully, as so often recently. She had decided to leave early the next morning, before most people were up; she would feel better once she was actually doing something. The inactivity, and the attempts at concentrating on her work, had been unbearable.

TWO

She got up as dawn was breaking, had breakfast, and made sure everything was tidy in the house. She had loaded all her supplies into the car over the last couple of days, so all she had to do was take out her holdall of clothes, lock up, and set off.

Her departure went unnoticed by most of her neighbours, and the one or two who did hear her car thought nothing of it. A few kilometres south, she turned left, on the main road towards the city, instead of heading the opposite way for the mountains. She felt tired, but it was a relief to be doing something. She had entered the coordinates of a point well south of Laxberg into the autopilot, and now engaged it so she could relax.

After an hour, the skyline of Laxberg came into view, and there was progressively more traffic on the road. She passed the familiar huge solar farms, and rows of giant wind turbines, turning gently against the blue sky, the blades flashing as they caught the sunlight. It was still quite early, so she decided to drive straight through the centre of town, rather than using the long and tedious orbital road. With luck, it would be a lot quicker.

As always, Dana felt oppressed by the enormous scale of the city. It was a vast sprawl, and the buildings in the central area were unbelievably tall. She quite enjoyed an occasional visit, but she was

glad that she lived in a rural area. The university campus was located in the northern suburbs, so she rarely had to go into central Laxberg. Luckily, driving through was straightforward, with wide boulevards and good signposting everywhere. She made good progress, and soon started seeing overhead signs for the Great Abyss. Once through the high-rise central area, she looked out for a convenient coffee shop, where she would be able to enjoy her last decent drink before heading into the unpopulated regions. There would be no tasty drink or food once she was in the wilds. She found a suitable place on the service road parallel to the main highway, and enjoyed a large coffee and a pastry, which revived her energy levels and alertness, then set off again for the empty quarter.

The suburbs of the city gradually thinned out either side of the H2 highway; more solar farms appeared, and soon the vegetation was becoming more sparse too, trees disappearing, and the landscape flattening out. The autopilot had beeped a warning at her, so she turned it off and assumed control of the truck. The node points built into the kerbs ran out somewhere around here, so that autopilots no longer functioned. Another hour later, she found herself in virtual desert country, albeit still quite green, with just scrubby vegetation scattered evenly over the mostly flat land, and just a slight undulation providing relief. There was only light traffic speeding in both directions now, much of it taking the form of vans or pick-up trucks. She stopped in a deserted lay-by, and got into the back of the truck to take a pee, keeping a look-out the whole time in case another vehicle should stop close to hers. But nothing at all passed while she was stopped. Before setting off again, she stood at the roadside and did a few stretching exercises. She decided to try her cellphone once more, but just heard the usual hiss and crackle. Yet there was good signal supposedly, since comms masts were still being maintained in this area; further south it would be a different story.

Dana set off again. She passed a rather demoralising large sign, announcing that the Great Abyss was 1,425 km ahead, and the Loir Rift 354 km. She would feel that she was beginning to make progress after she crossed the rather scary Rift Bridge. She would have to stop for the night soon after however.

The terrain was now largely flat as far as the eye could see, with just scattered large boulders and scrubby bushes punctuating the view. Dana played some of her favourite music to help while away the journey; luckily she had a plentiful supply in digital form, so she wouldn't run out.

There were one or two small settlements even this far south, but the last one was 100 km or more north of the Rift. The H2 highway passed these at some distance, to avoid the inhabitants having to put up with traffic noise. Dana would not be seeking a bed anywhere like this tonight; it would be bound to draw awkward questions from motel staff...

She ploughed on, the next small sign announcing 150 km remaining to the Rift. She covered the distance in just under an hour and a half. She was not sure how long ago she had last crossed the Rift Bridge, but it had to be at least 15 years; it had been during a trip with her parents, when she was a teenager. She had found the experience slightly scary at that time, but she had no time for nerves on this occasion. Nevertheless, she decided to turn off the highway and stop for a moment at the viewpoint; after all, this was one of the natural wonders of the planet, and she needed a break from driving.

Dana strolled from her truck to the guardrail on the viewing platform, and slowly looked down. Her breathing stopped for a moment as she took in the frightening prospect. The chasm stretched off into the distance, almost completely straight; below her, clouds floated deep in the Rift, and, far below, she could make out the glow of the flowing lava. There was an acrid, sulphurous smell, which caught at the back of the throat. She forced herself to take in the awesome spectacle for a few minutes, then returned quickly to her vehicle and moved off.

She rejoined the highway, and turned towards the bridge. Ahead, the road disappeared from view as it dipped over the edge of the chasm. She willed herself to stay calm; after all, this was a daily commuting route for some people, nothing to be frightened of. She accelerated, and the truck sped up, careering down the slope towards the low-point in the middle. It seemed terrifyingly deep; the guard-rails on either side seemed far too flimsy, and the far edge was high above

her now. She floored the accelerator, and the truck shot up the far slope, gradually losing momentum because of the steep gradient. At last, she felt less claustrophobic as the truck neared the far side, its speed greatly reduced as it reached the rim. Suddenly she was back at surface level, on solid flat ground, and wound her side window down to take in deep gulps of fresh air. She steadied her nerves, and told herself she must get a grip; there might be real hazards ahead, not just a flimsy-looking bridge...

She drove on. The daylight was dimming; it would be totally dark in forty minutes or so. There was hardly any other traffic on the road now, which was a bit unnerving in itself. This was normally a really busy highway, day and night. Suddenly, Dana spotted tail-lights far ahead. She had not come up behind another vehicle in the last couple of hours. It quickly became apparent that the vehicle ahead was stationery. Fifteen minutes later, she could make out a figure standing next to a small car, and she slowed down to work out what was happening ahead. Then she realised that the person by the car was facing her way, and waving. It was a young woman. Dana slowed to a stop behind the car, and the other woman strode over to her as she wound her side window down.

"Thank God you came along - thank you for stopping!" cried the stranger. "I've broken down, and I'm totally stuck... And I can't get a signal to call for help! Can you give me a lift?"

"Wait a minute," said Dana, "let's take a look at your car. What happened exactly?"

"There was a massive bang, and it just coasted to a stop... It just won't move at all now" replied the stranger.

Dana got out of her truck, and together they looked under the car's bonnet.

"I think the motor has fried" said the stranger. "The casing has cracked and half melted away!"

Dana could only agree. "But where are you going, and how come you're this far south alone?" she asked.

The stranger, whose name was Kim, initially seemed slightly reluctant to offer much of an explanation for her journey. But with a little encouragement, she quickly realised that there was no point in concealing any information; she explained how she too had lost all contact with her husband several weeks ago. His name was Calum, and he worked for the global water-supply company, Nor-Vatten. He had travelled to somewhere near Mandela to work on a feasibility study for a new aqueduct, and she had been unable to reach him, even since just before the start of the meteorite season. The police and authorities were not interested; they said that this happened every year at this time, and that people just had to wait for the all-clear, and for communications to be restored. But she knew perfectly well that the "season" never lasted this long, and felt certain that she was being fobbed off. So, like Dana, she had decided to take the bull by the horns, and drive half-way around the world to find her man. She had an added reason to want to contact Calum quickly: she had just learned that she was pregnant.

Dana's first reaction was to ask Kim if it was really a good idea to embark on this long and potentially hazardous journey while pregnant.

"I'm not ill!" she had replied. "It's a natural state for women; it doesn't mean I have to stay at home for nine months!"

"No, Of course not, I'm sorry; it's a natural protective reaction," Dana had said, rather defensively.

When Kim had finished her tale of woe, Dana related her own story, which was uncannily similar.

"OK," said Dana at last. "We can pool our resources, and travel together in my truck. It'll be good to have some company. But we need to get your car off the road first."

They moved everything portable and useful from Kim's car into the truck, then set about trying to move the car off the edge of the highway. In the end they had to haul it with a tow-rope; they decided to turn it around and leave it on the opposite side of the highway, so that it would look as though the driver was heading back to the city. They left it as far off the tarmac as they could, and locked it up. It would eventually be investigated, but they were fairly sure that the police would just assume, initially anyway, that the driver had been rescued by someone, and would arrange for a tow-truck to haul the car away in due course.

They drove off southwards again. It was dark, but Dana wanted to find a spot just off the road that would be concealed by boulders or vegetation, so that no-one would stop to check their vehicle during the night. They had not seen a single other vehicle in over an hour, but she really didn't want to start having a conversation with anyone about their presence in this forbidden location. The absence of traffic on the main H2 was beyond weird, she reflected; this road was supposed to always be really busy - even at night...

They soon found a suitable place, training a spotlight on the area to check for hidden dips or rocks, and bounced around a little as they moved into a very private looking saucer-shaped clearing. They got out of the truck to stretch again, listening out for any distant traffic that might be coming their way. There was almost total silence, with just a few insects chirruping here and there, and the most intensely bright star-scape above them. Dana had a momentary anxious thought about scorpions, but dismissed it as silliness. They were small, and their stings could be painful, but they caused no long-term harm.

The two women settled down to try and sleep in the truck, Dana in the front, and Kim on the back bench seat. It was quite constricted, but they were both physically and mentally exhausted; they curled up, and both soon fell into a deep sleep.

THREE

Dana woke with a start just as dawn was breaking. It took her a moment to remember where she was, and that she was sharing this small space with someone else. She eased herself up, and out of the truck quietly, and went to the back to find her camping stove and water jerrican. By the time she had it set up and lit, Kim was clambering out of the back seats, and looking around at their surroundings.

"Good morning!" she said. "You found us a great camping spot!"

"Morning! Yes, it seems quite well hidden. We were lucky to find it in the dark..."

They made some instant coffee and ate some sweet rolls, while discussing the day ahead, and how far they might realistically travel. They were about 600km from the Great Abyss, by Dana's reckoning. They should reach it by mid-afternoon, and then they would have to travel around its edge for some 300km before the highway headed further south, and towards the Arrif mountains. There was still no sound at all of human activity; they could probably have just parked by the side of the highway, but you could not be certain...

Having tidied up and had a cursory wash, they set off again across the undulating plain. It seemed hotter than on the previous day, but this was to be expected, as they were gradually getting closer to the tropics. The land was still scattered with small boulders here and there, and parched-looking bushes and cacti grew at intervals. Dana found herself liking this vast wilderness, devoid of pointless human pressures. Nevertheless, she felt a constant uneasiness and anxiety over what the coming days would bring, and whether she would be able to find Garth.

The two women found that they got along remarkably well. They were both quite easy-going, and had many tastes in common. Kim was a paramedic, it turned out, based at the Emergency Department of the biggest hospital in Laxberg. She was a petite brunette, with a tanned and pretty face, and clearly very fit. She loved long-distance running, and frequently took part in races. She was just coming up to her 30th birthday, a year younger than Dana. Dana enjoyed running too, although she hardly ever competed. They were both avid fans of White Star, one of the world's most famous bands, and both had attended several major concerts by them. Dana wondered at the unlikely scenario of the two of them finding each other as they had, and began to feel very grateful to have somebody to share this epic journey with.

After a couple of hours, they stopped briefly, and Kim took a turn at the wheel of the truck. Dana felt quite relieved to be able to just sit back and let someone else take control for a time. The road was good and smooth, but one still had to stay alert at all times. One hour further on, they spotted another vehicle in the distance, coming towards them. They became slightly tense, and discussed what they would do, and whether they would be expected to stop by the other driver. It turned out to be a non event. The other vehicle, a mid-sized van, just hurtled past them at speed, the driver giving a big wave and tooting his horn several times. They looked at each other in disbelief, then relaxed a little. But then, they began to wonder when the next occasion would come, and whether it would pan out so easily...

They were quiet for a while, then Dana spoke again.

"Do your parents know you're doing this trip?"

"It's just my mother. My father's no longer with us – he died a couple of years ago."

"Oh, I'm sorry to hear that..."

"Thanks... He'd been ill for around two years with a tumour in his brain, and just gradually faded away... It was horrible..."

"Oh, that's terrible... I'm so sorry... So did you tell your mother you were going to search for Calum?"

"Yes... And the amazing thing is that she was incredible! She didn't try to stop me – told me to go as soon as possible... I think that she was as worried as I was!"

"How amazing! She sounds like a strong woman."

"Yes, she definitely is. She's an inspiration to me..."

"How wonderful... It didn't go so well when I told my parents what I was going to do, I can tell you! But they accepted it in the end... I suppose they just had to... Anyway, tell me all about you and Calum, and why he went to Mandela."

"We've been together getting on for five years, and married for three," said Kim. "He's an engineer with Nor-Vatten, as I said before; we met at a friend's birthday party, and just hit it off. He's really kind and gentle - a caring type, you know... But strong too – quite a hunk! He was great when my father died - so understanding and supportive. My mother really loves him too. The only down-side to his job is that he often has to go on these field trips. They're usually in the north, and don't last so long up there, but he's come down to the Mandela area a few times. It's so much more arid down there, and less geologically stable, so they often have problems. They have engineers based down there permanently, but they seem to need reinforcement quite often. There's a major project being planned to build a water pipeline to serve Mandela from a bit further east, and that's what he's gone to do survey work for."

"That's a bit like with Garth," said Dana. "There was an earthquake close to Mandela about eight months back, and they're trying to figure a more reliable way of routing power cables, so they're not so vulnerable in future."

"Yes, it's not the safest area in the world," agreed Kim. "So, tell me more about Garth."

"Well, we've been married a couple of years; we got together almost two years before that. But we actually first met when we were in our teens; he's from the far south, and we met at one of those twinning summer camps they have every few years. I really liked him at the time, but I never imagined that we would end up together. He came to study at the university in Laxberg, and decided to stay in the north afterwards, even though his parents still live back in Dontsane."

The ties between the north and the far south had been greatly strengthened by camps organised by the two governments. They alternated in the two regions, and involved hundreds of youngsters travelling north or south on the seven-day road-train journey. The road-trains carried two hundred passengers in huge, comfortable and speedy coaches with trailers, equipped with the most sophisticated hydro-pneumatic suspension. The long-established trips had become a rite of passage for many young people.

"He's a really fun guy, quite impetuous I suppose. He's always great in company - the life and soul of the party, you know. I'm a bit more reserved, so I suppose he's brought me out of my shell slightly. People seem to be drawn to him somehow; he's always telling stories, and people gather round and listen to him, and want to know more. You'll like him, I'm sure! He loves exploring, so we've had one or two great trips together; but always up north, never into the desert regions. Although we did go down to the Great Abyss two years back. But he prefers the sea and the mountains really. He's never really enjoyed his assignments down south."

"Do you want children?"

"Oh yes... I'm not sure if Garth feels quite ready yet, but time is ticking along a bit now, and I think he realises that. So I hope it'll happen soon. I just need to find him again first!" added Dana, her face screwing up a little.

"We'll find them girl! We've got to keep positive. There's got to be a simple explanation for this..."

They stopped for a bite to eat from their supplies, and to drink some water, standing around at the side of the highway, in the shade of a large organ-pipe cactus, and admiring the unusual shrubs and cacti growing all around. There was a strange beauty to this landscape, which was so different from where they lived, but so endlessly empty.

A couple of hours later, they began to see a series of big tourist signs telling of the approaching Great Abyss, each one giving a tiny snippet of new information about this mysterious and gargantuan feature. The highway descended a gentle slope to a continuation of the previous landscape, but at slightly lower altitude. At last, they reached the section of the H2 which skirted the edge of the Abyss for some 300km, and soon came across the first of the numerous rest areas set up along the route. They turned onto the slip road to the parking lot, which was completely deserted.

Kim and Dana got out of the truck, and walked over to the viewing platform, which jutted out some 20 metres over the void. They had parked very close to it, in case they might feel the need to make a quick getaway, but there was just an eery silence bearing down on the place like an oppressive blanket. They reached the guard-rail, and peered down into the seemingly infinite depths. The Abyss gave the strangest feeling; it became progressively darker the deeper down one looked, as though light itself had difficulty escaping from the void below. Scattered clouds floated way below where they stood. The sound of their voices seemed strangely dead; the Abyss absorbed noises of any kind in the strangest way. It was easy to become disorientated, with sky seemingly above and below them, and so few points of reference for the senses. The Great Abyss had fascinated people for centuries, and given rise to numerous myths, but it was not a place that people wanted to stay near. The two women very soon felt this way themselves, and returned gratefully to the enveloping cosiness of their truck.

They pressed on, eager to cover more distance, casting slightly nervous glances over towards the Abyss from time to time. They passed more rest areas, deserted every time, but did not stop. Dana was aware that one of the last of these areas had some public facilities, which she hoped would not have been locked up. She looked forward to seeing a man-made structure again, after nearly two days in the wilderness.

Much later, a larger rest area with sizeable buildings hove into view, and they turned down the slip-road to it, eager to discover whether there would be anything useful to them here. The parking lots were deserted again, so they drove right up to the biggest building, which appeared to house a cafeteria and fast-food outlets. Unsurprisingly, everything was closed up, but there were vending machines which seemed in working order, and it looked as though there were wash-rooms which might be operational.

They decided to see if they could charge up the truck's power cells from one of the public points, then they would investigate the wash-rooms. They were fairly confident that the charging points would be working, and so it turned out. The site was surrounded by a solar farm, so power was always being generated; it would be pointless disconnecting the charging stations, since there could always be emergency vehicles needing them. Kim inserted her payment card into the machine, while Dana plugged in the cable. It was a relief to charge up the truck while they had the chance.

They ambled back to the main buildings with wash-bags and towels, hopeful that there was still water remaining in the adjacent tower. Just as they were reaching the building, a vehicle drove in off the slip-road. It was a police car.

Dana and Kim stood rooted to the spot. They could hardly run away, or race back to their truck. They had clearly been seen, and it would be pointless trying to outrun a police car...

The cops drove straight across to where the women stood, and the two officers got out of their vehicle and strode over to them.

"Good afternoon, ladies. And what brings you out here today?" inquired the older of the two cops, a sergeant, looking rather stern.

"We're just touring, officer" replied Dana, trying to sound as matter-of-fact as possible.

"In meteorite season?" asked the cop bluntly, as his colleague rolled his eyes.

"It's more peaceful" said Kim.

"Well ladies, I'm sure you know that you're not supposed to come into Meteorite Alley during the closed season, so I have to advise you to return to a place of safety as soon as possible. And just so you know, we're supposed to give a five thousand Kroner fine to anyone driving south of the Loir Rift at this time! Now, I get the distinct feeling that you're not telling me everything, so please explain to me in full the real reason you're here, and where you've come from!"

Dana and Kim felt crestfallen; they looked at each other sheepishly, and decided simultaneously that they would spill their story. They would probably be escorted away from the area anyway, so what was there to lose by concealing anything?

They told the cops that they were trying to reach Mandela, because their husbands seemed to be missing, and comms were non-existent, way beyond the normal end of the meteorite storms. They had been unable to gain any information or help from the authorities in the capital. All they wanted to do was just drive to the far south to try and find out what had happened to their loved ones. Was that so unreasonable?

The sergeant looked at his junior, blew out his cheeks, and exhaled with a puff.

"You must be out of your minds!" he stated baldly. "It's over 12,000 kilometres from Laxberg to Mandela! Are you sure that your vehicle is up to that? Can you recharge your cells sufficiently?"

Dana assured him that her truck was in top condition; she had looked into the availability of power on the journey, and had also invested in several portable hydrogen plug-in power-cells as back-up.

"Well now," he said, "we're supposed to make sure that nobody drives through here and into dangerous territory, but I understand your reasons, and it makes little difference to us personally what you do, although we're supposed to protect you. Of course, we might have missed you if we'd driven off on that side road back there anyway, so maybe we never saw you..." The last statement was accompanied by a little grin.

The women stared at the cops and swallowed, but stayed silent.

"My feeling is that the meteorite shower has indeed largely passed," continued the sergeant, "so that you're unlikely to get a problem from that direction. As long as your vehicle has adequate power and you have suitable equipment, I don't think that you are in danger from nature."

"Wait a minute," said Kim, "do I get the impression that you think there is some - *different* kind of danger abroad?"

"Well, I don't rightly know, Ma'am. We don't get a lot of news out here, but I can't quite figure why the all-clear for these highways hasn't been announced yet. It seems kinda odd... It's never been this late before..."

"So... You're not going to make us drive back to the city?" asked Dana hesitantly.

"I'm just being realistic, Ma'am. I can't spend two to three days escorting you back to Laxberg. You might give us the slip in the night anyway. I would strongly recommend that you turn back, but it's hard for us to enforce. You look capable types, and you seem to have some knowledge of what you're letting yourselves in for. I would just plead with you to be mighty careful. But I will give you my cell number, in the hope that signal returns soon, in case you run into any trouble in the next day or so. After that, you're absolutely on your own... We will deny all knowledge of having ever seen you..."

The women thanked the officers profusely, and assured them that they would be careful. The cops returned to their car and drove away with friendly waves.

"Well, that was slightly odd," said Dana, "what on earth is going on, I wonder?"

"I don't know," replied Kim. " They seemed like really decent guys; they were just concerned for our safety. But why exactly, I can't quite work out. I don't think that meteorites are a threat now. But they didn't seem to know if something else weird is happening..."

They went back to checking out the wash-rooms. To their great delight, they found the showers fully functional, with warm water too. They decided afterwards that they might as well stay the night here, as it was nearly dark. The cops knew of their existence, so they wouldn't trouble them again, and the truck's batteries would get a full charge.

FOUR

They both felt a bit more refreshed the following morning. It had been revitalising to enjoy a good shower, and they had managed to sleep a little better, despite the cramped conditions in the truck. They had some breakfast, and enjoyed another wash before setting off again. The truck had enough charge to keep them going for at least a couple of days, and they still had the extra plug-in power cells too. Dana began to feel a bit more confident that they could reach their destination without problem.

The H2 continued along the rim of the Abyss for some distance, with the occasional deserted rest areas still punctuating the journey. There were few facilities in these however; they were just parking lots, and maybe a viewing platform with information boards. But there was one major landmark around 150km further on, and that was the Lava Falls. At this point, the highway passed over a wide and deep rift, at the bottom of which flowed another lava river. Just past the bridge, slip roads led off to a visitor centre and viewing platforms, where tourists stopped in great numbers - in normal times - to take in the awesome spectacle of the Falls. Here, the lava stream hurled itself over the brink and into the Great Abyss. The void below seemed so vast that it could swallow any amount of molten magma dropping in from the rift. It probably came back to

the surface later, in an extraordinary circular movement, but this was not proven for certain.

Dana and Kim decided that they might as well stop off at the Falls, take a short break, and swap driving duties. As they passed over the bridge, they could see that the parking areas at the Falls were deserted once again. They drove close to the viewing platform area, and got out of the truck to take a quick look. It seemed impossible to come to this extraordinary place without admiring the scene. It would not delay their journey by very much.

They reached close to the substantial guard-rails, but dithered a moment before going right up to them. The heat was overpowering, and wafts of sulphurous fumes drifted towards them every few seconds, making them gasp and cough, and their eyes water. They peered down over the edge, watching large dollops of lava separating from the surprisingly liquid flow, and plummeting soundlessly into the great void. The heat on their faces was almost painful, so they soon turned away to return to the truck, rendered speechless for a few minutes by the outlandish spectacle.

They were able to use the bathrooms outside the visitor centre before setting off again, as well as buying some large bottles of water from the vending machines. The big complex was eerily quiet, and this felt very disconcerting somehow, so they were glad to get moving again on the open road.

* * *

The H2 highway soon turned away from the edge of the Abyss, heading due south again. The landscape reverted to the earlier flatness, with scrubby vegetation and cacti. The next major landmark would be the Arrif Mountains, 500km or so further on. But before reaching the highlands, they would have to pass through the great expanse of Crater Plain.

After 60 - 70 kilometres of lightly undulating terrain, the land flattened out again, and the vegetation grew more sparse. They began to pass small impact craters. 'Small' in relative terms, that is. They were rarely less than 100 metres across, and some could be three or four times that diameter. It was clear that the impacts caused by these meteorites hitting the surface would have been colossal. On a couple of occasions, the highway took an extensive diversion around a big crater, evidence that the road had taken a direct hit from a meteorite at some time in the past. Huge signs with arrows in luminous paint gave ample warning of the change to the road. Dana found herself quite spooked by the scale of the craters they passed.

"Can you imagine what it would be like to be around here when a meteorite strikes?" she asked Kim.

"I'd rather not try to think about it!" replied her companion. "It would be terrifying... Can you imagine the noise, and the blast?"

"Not really... Well, let's hope the season really is over, because there's no place much to hide out here!"

Luckily of course, the trajectory of the belt of rocks which came down to earth each year as meteorites had been well plotted by now. The timing of the meteorite shower was quite accurately predicted, and they normally only came down in this central desert belt of the planet. There had been a few famous exceptions to the rule of course, but they were very rare. But now, here was this unusual situation, in which the all-clear had not been announced, three weeks after its normal time, and communications with the south were apparently non-existent. It was very strange.

A few kilometres ahead, they could see a column of smoke slanting away from a fresh-looking crater. The meteorite which struck this spot had evidently found a very thin point in the earth's crust, in this geological fault region. The impact would have crashed through the crust, and made magma fly in all directions in a horrendous explosion. The lava would slowly set, and plug the hole once more. A couple of similar, slightly older craters could be seen in the distance on either side, with just a faint wisp of smoke rising from each.

The two young women drove on. They suddenly realised that the Arrif Mountains had come into sight; a very faint grey-blue silhouette on the horizon. As they pressed on, the shape acquired more solidity, and they began to make out peaks and valleys within the whole. By early afternoon, the mountains seemed quite close,

and they realised that they formed a much bigger obstacle on their route than they had hitherto believed.

The surface of the road had been excellent so far, surprisingly. It was remarkable that the highway was so well maintained, in view of the distances it covered. But this happy state was not to last. They reached a stretch of road where large potholes had formed, and the tarmac was markedly rutted. The noise level inside the truck rose to an unpleasant level, as the tyres ran over the increasingly rough surface, and flung loose stones up onto the inside of the wheel arches. The ruts sometimes caught the tyres, forcing the truck onto even worse areas. The truck bounced in and out of holes in the surface, and they had to slow to a relative crawl to avoid damage. It was a frustrating situation, and there seemed to be no visible end to this section. They continued cautiously, praying that the road would return to its previous smooth state, while fearing that the bad stretch would continue endlessly. After negotiating a particularly bad section, which had jolted them around quite uncomfortably, Dana decided to stop briefly for a rest.

The two of them got out of the truck, and stretched their legs a little. Dana went to the back of the truck, and unclipped the tilt covering the cargo area, to make sure that everything was undamaged from the rough ride. She was horrified and infuriated to see that the most recently-opened water container was lying on its side, and the contents had all poured away, draining out onto the road. She called out angrily to her companion.

"Kim! You didn't secure the jerrycan, and didn't replace its cap properly, you stupid mare!"

Kim rushed across to see the damage for herself, trying to recall her actions from earlier on.

"I told you – you must ALWAYS secure ALL the containers with the bungee cords! And why the hell didn't you put the cap back on it?" Dana continued.

"Oh, Dana... I'm so sorry! I must have just forgotten... Oh, no... I'm so stupid... I don't know how I did it..." Kim felt terrible at being responsible for losing so much of their precious water. She could not quite remember how she had managed to forget to secure the thing. "Will we have enough left?"

"Well, I don't know... We don't have enough for the whole trip, that's for sure. We'll just have to hope that we can pick up some more somewhere, won't we. Now come on, let's get moving again," she said, with an exasperated tone.

They got back in the truck, Dana rushing to move off before Kim had had time to fasten her seat-belt. Kim sat silently, feeling very upset and belittled. She went over their departure that morning, trying to remember how she might have forgotten to put the cap back on the container, and then turned her mind to Dana's angry reaction to the incident. She could not quite figure why Dana was being so unpleasant; it had so clearly been an unfortunate oversight. She obviously would not deliberately put their water supply in jeopardy... The longer she thought about the incident, the more upset she became, until the point when she buried her face in her hands, and started to sob uncontrollably.

Dana had been driving along with a forced concentration, her eyes angrily fixed on the road ahead, when she suddenly became aware of Kim's distress. She looked round, saw Kim crying, and brought the truck to a halt again. Her heart melted at the sight of her new friend being so upset.

"Oh, Kim... I'm sorry... I didn't mean to upset you like that... I don't know what came over me. I don't normally take it out on people like that..." She leaned over and put her arms around Kim, then wiped the tears from her cheek. "Oh God... I think it's just the tension of this situation... I'm sorry..."

"It's OK, thank you..." Kim whispered. "I'll try not to do anything stupid again!"

"Oh... Please, don't worry... It could have been me just as easily. And I'm sure that we'll be able to get water at some roadside place. There are often vending machines. I'm so sorry for being so horrible..."

"It's all right... I understand."

"Listen," said Dana, "I can't tell you how glad I am that you're here with me. This trip would be unbearable if I were on my own..."

"Thanks, Dana. Yes, I have to say, I'm kind of glad that my car broke down. I'm not sure how far I would have got on my own..."

" Well, I'll try not to be mean again. I promise. We've got to look after each other..."

"Yes, agreed. OK, thanks, let's carry on."

They got under way again, both feeling a bit better, friends once more, although Dana felt very badly for having upset Kim so much. She resolved to try and keep a grip on her emotions. Unfortunately, the poor road surface continued. The terrain had taken on a slow undulation again, so that they would briefly enjoy a wide vista over a huge open area, before descending again into a long dip, and feeling cut off from the rest of the world. Then the highway's surface quite suddenly became billiard-table smooth again, making them both exclaim with relief at the return of the blissful quietness and lack of vibration.

They were just coming up to the crest of a very slight rise, when suddenly a flash of red, accompanied by a high-pitched droning whine, swept past them in the opposite direction, the loud note rising abruptly and then lowering and fading as it receded behind them. Kim jumped out of her skin at the unexpectedness of it, and Dana twitched visibly too.

"A despatch motor-cycle!" she stated. "It's the only way they can send news up north if there's a comms shut-down..."

A small team of elite riders was employed to take despatches north and south during the meteorite season, which was usually also accompanied by communications-destroying solar flare activity. They were buccaneering young men and women, who were regarded as heroic for their apparent disregard of the danger to their own lives when riding through the central desert belts during the 'season'. They rode the iconic red Triumph motorcycles, and wore matching red head-to-toe outfits. They took precedence over any other kind of traffic, particularly when reaching the city areas of their destination. They rode at ridiculous speeds, and covered the distance from Mandela to Laxberg in a mere four days, stopping only for the shortest time possible for human endurance. This meant riding for a gruelling sixteen or even eighteen hours per day. The large panniers mounted at the back carried extra hydrogen cells, the despatches themselves being held in tiny digital memory sticks. Two riders had died in the previous five years, but there was never a shortage of volunteers for this prestigious job.

"So, there is still some kind of news getting through!"

"Yes," agreed Kim, "but precious few details to do with missing persons, I'm guessing..."

"I wonder..." said Dana. "You don't think that we've been too impetuous in doing this trip, do you? We might have just flashed past the very news we're waiting for..."

"I don't know... It's possible I suppose. But I just couldn't bear to sit around waiting any longer. And if the news does arrive in Laxberg, how soon would they let us know about Calum and Garth? And would there be that much detail about individuals in the report anyway, or would it just be generalities about events down south?"

"You're probably right. I think we'll get a lot more information when we get to the other end, and maybe even find the guys soon after. The authorities back home are so slow to pass on news..." observed Dana. There was a nagging little element of doubt in her mind, but she did not want to express it out loud. She resolved to try and drive faster.

The flat plain seemed to end very abruptly, and suddenly they were climbing up a steep slope; and then the great highway became slightly narrower, and began to wind its way upwards in an unending series of hair-pin bends. The slopes became greener, with fir trees gradually covering the ground more and more. They stopped in a big wide lay-by, and studied their maps, and got out of the truck to admire the view back over Crater Plain. The sky was clear, and the scene was almost idyllic; they could have been on a holiday tour, were it not for the anxiety they both felt deep down. That, and the mysterious total absence of other traffic... Taking a closer look at the fir trees, they were astonished to see how they appeared to take root in solid rock... Roots would run along the ground for a few metres sometimes, before finding a fissure to delve into for moisture. They spotted a number of large lizards basking in sunny patches.

Dana took the wheel again, and they got back under way. The road continued to climb and wind. It was an extraordinary engineering feat, with viaducts spanning valleys, and tunnels piercing through mountains, climbing relentlessly all the time. Dana had heard that some of the tunnels were very long, and she felt a little apprehensive about this. Would the lights be on for the full length, she wondered; and could there be any unwelcome surprises up here? They saw the occasional evidence of a meteorite strike, with trees flattened and charred in a big area, but the road appeared to be intact, so far.

They came to their first long tunnel. This one was a straight affair, and they could see the dot of bright light at the far end. The lights were working fine inside the tunnel; as they were powered by solar panels, in theory they were never turned off, and banks of batteries kept them going through the night. The only fear was that a meteorite strike might wipe out the power supply...

They emerged from the tunnel to blinding sunlight, and carried on up the mountainside. They were high above the plain now, but still going up. The road hugged the side of the slope, curving into valleys and out again. Sometimes they would catch a glimpse of the road at a much higher level, way above the point where they were travelling. On one such occasion they suddenly saw that, far ahead, the road dived into a massive cave, formed naturally rather than excavated by humans. The extraordinary sight made the two women gasp simultaneously. A few minutes later, they were approaching the mouth of this strange feature. Dana instinctively slowed down as they entered the cavern. It was a slightly unnerving sight. The roof was invisible, lost in the darkness of this vast space; in this instance, lights had been installed at very low level, just knee-height above the tarmac along the roadway. The road curved slowly to the right as it went through, but the far end quickly came into view, much to their relief.

Once again, they were dazzled by the bright daylight when the road emerged from the cavern. But they began to feel less nervous; the roads appeared to be in good order so far, with the lighting working perfectly. There seemed to be nothing to worry about. Even so, they would drive through the tunnels at a moderate speed, just in case.

The next tunnel came into sight; it looked like nothing out of the ordinary. But, just as they were entering the mouth, two mid-sized white panel vans shot out of the entrance, hurtling down the mountain in the opposite direction. Both women shrieked out, and Dana inadvertently swerved to avoid the vans which were no longer there; she quickly regained control of herself and their truck, but they were left freaked out by this unexpected meeting. Dana looked in the rear-view mirror every few seconds, convinced that the other vehicles would turn around to pursue them, but nothing came into sight, and all remained clear up ahead. They asked each other what this could mean, and who the other road-users could have been, but no logical explanation offered itself. They decided to stop at the very next lay-by, and try to find whether any other vehicles could be heard in the distance.

They found a parking spot quite soon, and stopped gratefully. They both got out of the truck, closing the doors as quietly as possible, and strained their ears to hear the slightest sound. Nothing whatsoever could be detected. There was just an eery silence. High above them, a group of large raptors soared in thermal updraughts.

"Well, that was strange", said Dana.

"Yes... But then, if we're here, then I suppose that other people can be too..."

"Yeah. I was kind of getting used to us being the only ones around, but I suppose we're bound to run into somebody sooner or later... I wonder where they had come from?"

The women took in the view once again. They were at quite a high altitude by now - maybe 1,500 to 2,000 metres, and the temperature was very pleasant here, after the crushing earlier heat of the plain. Having listened out carefully for any sounds of human activity for a few minutes, they decided to get back on the road, with Kim taking the wheel. The two had bonded well by now, despite the little spat earlier that day, which Dana still felt bad about. They had tastes in common, as well as being in the same situation with regard to their menfolk; they had begun to feel like old friends.

The highway continued climbing, but they could see that they would reach a high point or a pass before long. They passed over more viaducts, and rounded hairpin bends. The trees became sparser at this altitude, and bare rock surfaces were the main features, with an

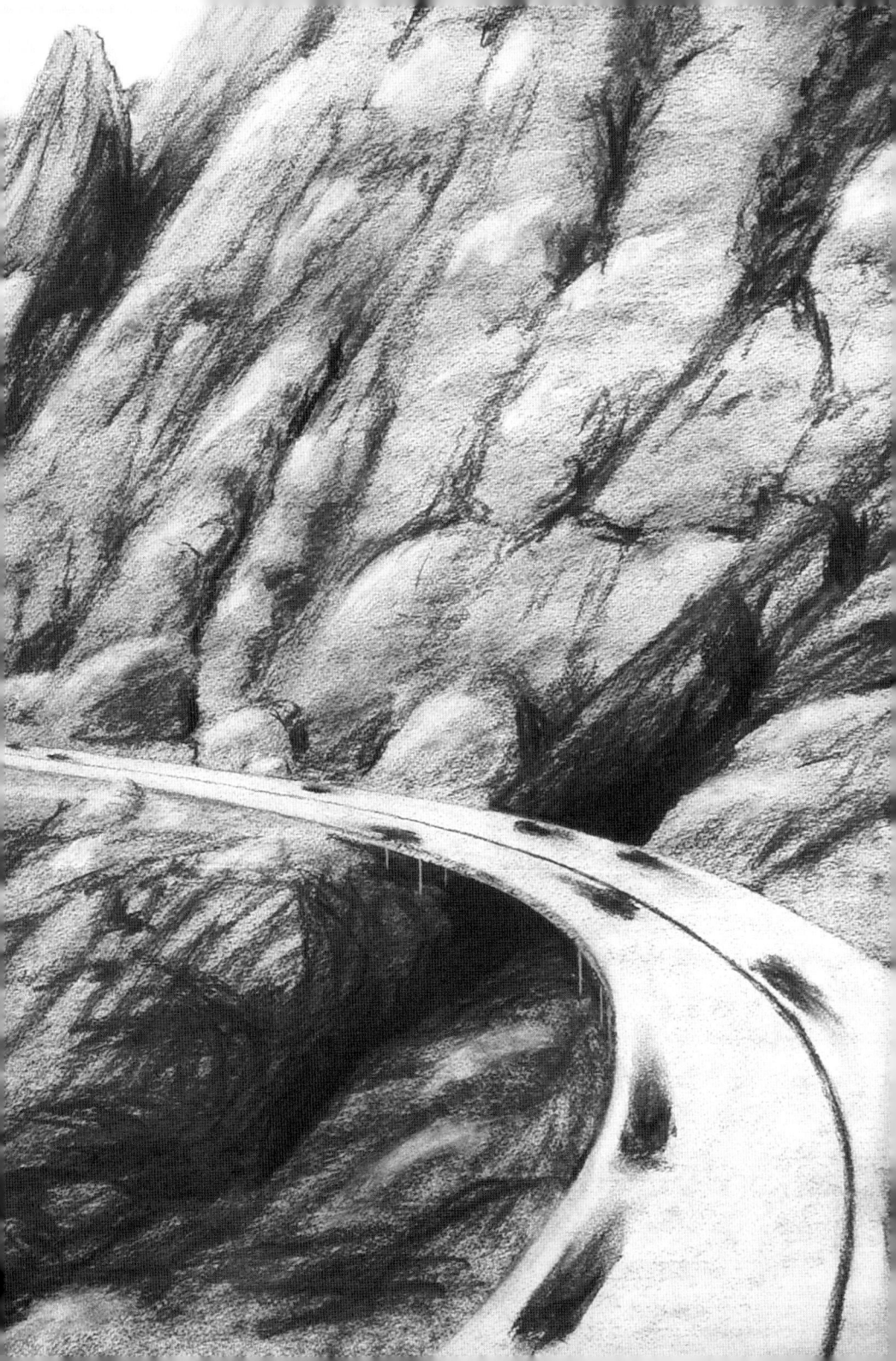

occasional cactus type plant. The road flattened out, and they suddenly caught a glimpse of the plain to the south of the mountains. They had reached the highway's highest point, and could see the horizon 60 kilometres in either direction. They passed a viewpoint with numerous parking spaces, but drove on, feeling the need to cover more distance.

They began to descend the southern flank of the Arrif range; this side appeared to be almost a mirror-image of the ground they had covered on the way up, with perhaps slightly fewer tunnels, as they discovered. A couple of hours later, they were approaching the start of the Ighazar plains. They were almost one third of the way through their journey.

The H2 highway became arrow-straight once again, as it disappeared into the distance, due south. The terrain was flatter than before, and more sandy, and with fewer plants than north of the mountains. At first, stunted acacia and wormwood trees dotted the land, but these soon petered out, giving way to clumps of grass and small succulents. The heat was oppressive, although it was quite dry, which made it a bit more bearable. They noticed that a bank of cloud seemed to be building up to the east, just over the horizon, but possibly coming their way very slowly. The rest of the sky was an even, clear blue.

Just then, they came across another unexpected stretch of road with a poor surface. Mercifully, it was quite short. But, just as they were about to return to a well-maintained smooth surface again, the truck dropped into a pot-hole with a jarring jolt. The hole had not seemed at all significant, but it was surprisingly deep and steep-sided. As they speeded up following the rough patch, a horrible throbbing sound came from the back end of the truck, which began vibrating horribly.

"What the hell's happened?" asked Kim, slowing down. The noise and the vibration stopped as they slowed right down, but began again as soon as Kim tried increasing their speed.

"Oh, no... I don't believe it!" Said Dana. "We'd better stop and see what's wrong..."

Kim stopped the truck at the edge of the road, and they got out to look all round the vehicle. Dana almost immediately spotted that the rear right wheel-rim was buckled from its impact with the edge of the pot-hole. The tyre was a bit damaged too, but had not deflated, as most tyres had partial foam-filling nowadays.

"This wheel is bent..." she said to Kim. "It's undoubtedly that causing the vibration..."

"Do we have a spare wheel?" asked Kim.

"Yes, it's underneath the cargo area here, together with the jack and tools. Well, this should be interesting!"

"At least it didn't happen in that mountain area," said Kim.

"No, that's a bit of luck, I suppose. OK, give me a hand here, would you?"

They lifted the surprisingly heavy spare wheel out of its cubby after moving some of the contents of the cargo bay, and tried to figure out how and where to fit the jack. Dana wound the handle, and the rear wheel raised just off the ground. There were five nuts holding the wheel on to its hub. She fitted the wrench to the first nut, and tried turning it. The whole wheel turned, making it impossible to loosen the nut.

"Wait a minute, we need to lower the tyre back onto the road enough to stop it rotating..." Dana said.

They lowered the truck slightly, and tried the wrench again. It was too stiff to turn...

"Do we have a hammer or mallet of any kind?" asked Kim.

"Yes! I'm pretty sure that Garth keeps something in here somewhere. Let's just take a look at the tool compartment again."

They found a small hammer, and gave the wrench a smart whack. The nut freed with a slight cracking sound, and Dana was able to unscrew it all the way. The next three nuts came undone with a similar treatment. Just one to go. She fitted the wrench to the last nut, and gave the end of its handle a sharp crack. Nothing happened. She tried twice more, but the nut refused to budge. It was well and truly seized on.

"You try, Kim..." she said.

Kim tried the same method, but without success.

"Oh, God! What are we going to do?" cried Dana. "Normally, you just stand by the roadside looking helpless, and a bunch of guys stop and fight each other to help you! And here we are with not a soul within a thousand kilometres!"

"Wait a minute," said Kim, "what we need is some penetrating oil..."

"Oh yes? And do you just happen to have to have some of that in your handbag?"

"No... But maybe we can mix up something similar. Do you have any EDT?"

"EDT? What the hell is that?"

"You know, perfume! *Eau de toilette*! Or else nail-polish remover?"

"Oh, right... I might have a tiny bottle of something... But what good will that do, apart from giving us a beautifully-scented wheel-nut?"

"Well, I remember Calum telling me about this fix: if we can mix a little oil with a bit of EDT, it can make a substitute for penetrating oil that's even better than the real thing!"

"Oh, wow! Well, it's worth a shot... Let's see what we can find..."

"A vegetable oil would do just as well – you know, the culinary kind..."

They searched through their personal bags, the truck's equipment, and even their food supplies. Dana found a little bottle of eau de toilette. Oil was being elusive, there being no engine oil dipstick on their electric vehicle. Looking again through their mobile larder, Kim came across an old sachet of salad cream lurking in the bottom of a box. It was well past its sell-by date, but that would not matter. It was at least 22% vegetable oil, which might do the trick. She took one of their small camping cups, and mixed a little of the salad cream with a good dose of the perfume, until she had a suitable-looking thin oily mixture. She spooned the substance onto the recalcitrant wheel-nut, a little at a time.

"Right," said Kim, "let's leave that to soak in for a few minutes. If nothing else, as you said, we'll have the most gorgeous smelling wheel-nut!"

"How long does it need to take effect?" asked Dana.

"I don't rightly know... Let's wait ten minutes, then try it..."

They waited anxiously, staring at the wheel, willing their makeshift mixture to soak through the offending rust. Kim spooned a tiny bit more on. Then she refitted the wrench, and they prepared to apply their strength to it. Kim took the hammer, and gave the end of the wrench a bang. She thought that maybe it moved, just a tiny bit.

"Hit it again!" said Dana.

She hit it again. This time it moved a little more.

"Yes! I think it's budging!" cried Kim triumphantly.

She struck the end of the wrench again, and this time it moved much further. She then applied as much weight as possible to the tool, and the nut slowly started turning. A few seconds later, it was unscrewing freely.

"Oh, well done Kim! That was genius! Thank God... I had visions of us sitting here for days, just waiting for someone to come along..."

"That went better than I had hoped, I must admit. I think I'll just drip the last of this stuff onto all the threads, just in case we need to undo them again."

"OK, but we don't have another spare wheel, so we're going to have to hope we get no more problems... It just illustrates how we're on our own out here. We've got to be self-reliant..." said Dana.

"Yes, well, the odds of us having another similar problem are pretty low. It's amazing really that the wheel rim bent; they're so heavy-duty on this truck. But we obviously need to keep our eyes skinned for this kind of hazard..."

They took the bent wheel off, and fitted the spare, then tidied everything away, and cleaned their hands as best they could. They both felt exhausted from the physical exertion as well as the tension of the situation, but they could not stop and rest.

They pressed on at speed, anxious to cover some distance after the enforced stop, and the earlier slow, winding mountain section. But now their eyes constantly scanned the road surface anxiously. Up ahead, they noticed some strange formations coming into view in the far distance. They looked like columns of rock, small in area, like old volcanic plugs, jutting vertically upwards to a considerable height. Half an hour later, they were getting close to the first of these, which the highway passed remarkably near to. They figured out that it must be an old volcanic core; it was huge, maybe 300 metres tall, and a small wisp of cloud seemed to be hovering alongside the top of it on the shady side. There seemed to be a dry river-bed meandering away from the base, and suddenly they found themselves crossing a red-painted rigid metal bridge over the desiccated stream. The stony river bed stretched away for maybe a kilometre, and then just seemed to fade away. They slowed down slightly as they passed the monolith, peering curiously at it, but didn't stop, even though a big rest area beckoned travellers invitingly.

A little further on, there was a curious sign by the roadside, simply marked "SHELTER". Shelter from what? they wondered. A slip-road diverged from the highway soon after, and seemed to dive underground. A similar road led off the north-bound lane, and also disappeared below ground. It was puzzling.

"There's some local knowledge around here that we're not party to," said Dana.

"Seems that way," agreed Kim.

Then came the strangest sight so far. The women had seen another monolith in the distance, but this one seemed from far off to be anvil-shaped. As they got closer, the detail gradually came into focus, and they realised that they were looking at the hulk of an ancient rusting cargo ship, perched atop a volcanic plug, its back broken. Kim suddenly remembered having read about this, years ago; she had forgotten about its existence. This time, they did stop, briefly. It was just the oddest thing, and they had trouble imagining what could have happened in this area, for a sea to totally dry out, and presumably with little warning... On closer examination, they realised that what they had thought were areas of scattered stones, were actually sea-shells, clumped together in patches. Looking into the distance, they noticed that a couple of other ships were visible far away, equally stranded on dry land, although not perched on a pedestal like this one.

Dana took the wheel again, and they resumed the journey. It was late afternoon now, so they would have to look out for somewhere safe to stop. They passed another "SHELTER" sign, and wondered again what it meant. They resolved to turn off and investigate if they came across another one. The plain continued, seemingly endless. More curious monoliths appeared. The cloud bank over to the east had greatly increased in size, but it was still bright and sunny over the H2.

45 minutes later, another sign loomed up ahead, and sure enough, it was marked "SHELTER". Dana slowed down, and turned onto the slip-road. They both felt slightly nervous, and sat forward in their seats, at high alert. The road dived below ground, and Dana slowed to a crawl, ready to stop and reverse at speed all the way back up the slip-road, if necessary. They dipped under a roof structure, and overhead lights suddenly began turning on, activated by motion sensors. The gloom lit up, and they found themselves in a huge, totally empty underground car park. At the far end, they could see the exit road, leading back up to the surface. To one side, there were signs leading to wash-rooms.

"Well, how civilised is this?" said Kim.

"Yes, but I can't figure out why they went to the trouble of excavating all this, instead of just building on the surface," answered Dana. "I know it's hot up there, but it was much the same to the north of the mountains. It just doesn't make any sense..."

"I know, but look - why don't we make use of this while we can? If we're lucky again, there might be running water in there," she said, pointing towards a set of doors to one side.

"I suppose. But I do find this place a bit creepy..."

"I know, but we're both dog-tired, and we don't know when we'll next find somewhere good to stop."

"True enough. Maybe it'd be good if we parked close to the exit ramp. That way we can make a quick getaway if someone comes and spooks us."

They agreed on this plan, and went together to check out the wash-rooms. Once again, incredibly, everything was working normally;

the lights came on, and there was warm water in the taps. Dana observed that it was probably a whole lot harder to have cold water than warm, in this particular location.

They used the facilities together, and walked back through the echoing car park together, neither of them feeling secure enough to go anywhere alone in this strange place. They ate and drank, and settled down for the night, locking all the doors securely. The overhead lights went out one by one, sensing no movement. At least the lights would alert them if anyone else entered the shelter. There was just a slight, comforting glow of lightness coming from the entrance and exit ramps, but even this turned pitch-black after a time.

Tired though she was, it took Kim some time to fall asleep. She lay on her side, curled in a foetal position, reflecting on the day. It had been arduous, both physically and emotionally, but it had ended on a high note. Following the very unfortunate incident with the spilled drinking water, she had eventually proved her worth by freeing the seized wheel-note. There was no doubt about it, she had saved the day, if not the entire trip. Kim had begun her journey with Dana very much as the junior partner, but their relationship was becoming more of a partnership of equals.

FIVE

Kim awoke with a start, hours later. The dim glow of early morning was filtering down the access ramps, but something else was odd. She realised that it was a strange sound that had disturbed her. She opened a door slightly, and heard an odd, low howling noise. She shook Dana awake.

"Dana! There's something weird going on out there!" she cried anxiously.

Dana came round from a deep sleep almost instantly, and listened, concentration etched over her face. She opened a door of the truck, and some of the overhead lights turned on. She couldn't see anything wrong. They put their shoes on, and walked towards the exit ramp.

"What the hell is that sound?" cried Kim.

"No idea. Let's just go a little closer to the ramp..."

They reached the bottom of the exit ramp, still below the overhanging roof. Looking out, they could see that the sky was an odd-looking slate grey colour, streaked with lighter bands. They took a few more steps up the ramp, then a few more, until they had a view of almost half the sky overhead.

"My God! It's a twister!" cried Kim suddenly. "Quick, get back to the truck! Oh, hell, I'm going to be sick!" Dana glanced at her quickly, and noticed that her face was deathly pale.

They ran back to the truck, slammed the doors firmly shut, and Dana started the motor. She drove towards the centre of the shelter, then close to the side wall, the furthest she could get away from the access ramps. They sat tensely, listening and waiting. Most of the overhead lights had come on, but now some of them were flickering on and off worryingly. The howling sound became louder and louder, added to which there was also a deeper, rushing sound. The howling reached a fever pitch. The women realised that the wind was acting on the shelter entrance, in a bigger version of blowing across the neck of an open bottle, but it was still the most terrifying noise. Then the air in the underground space was throbbing rhythmically in the most uncomfortable way, making them both clap their hands over their ears. Thick dust abruptly billowed in through the exit for some twenty seconds or so, rushing through to the entrance in an almost solid-looking stream, then swirled around the space, slowly settling.

Then the sound volume was reducing, and the two women relaxed a little.

"I think it's passed over," said Dana.

"Let's hope so!" Kim replied. But then she abruptly opened her door, leaned over, and threw up. "I'm sorry," she said, "I think it's just morning sickness..."

"Oh, you poor thing! Just sit back, and breathe easy for a minute. We're safe enough in here."

"Maybe, but I don't like this place much! I'll be fine in a minute..."

They sat still a little longer, then decided to drive back close to the exit ramp, and see what they could see. Some of the rows of lights were staying dark now, but a few came on. Looking out, they could see that the sky's colour had lightened considerably, though it was still banded grey.

They got out of the truck, and walked slowly up the ramp, looking all around as they went. Nearing the top, they suddenly caught sight of the milky-coloured sloping column of the tornado, already a few kilometres away, and travelling away from them at speed. There was debris strewn all around, evident even in this desert landscape. Broken fragments of solar panel were lying in strange positions, together with large rocks, some of these dumped on the highway itself. They would have to take extra care when they drove out of here, that was for sure. Looking eastwards, the sky was clearing, so they hoped that they would not have to run the gauntlet of further twisters.

"I guess we've discovered what the shelters are for!" said Kim, who seemed to have regained her normal colour.

"Yes. I had been thinking that they probably wouldn't withstand a meteorite strike, but couldn't figure out what the hell they were built for. Tornados must be regular events around here."

"Well, let's hope we don't see any more!"

They went back underground, and took the truck back close to the wash-rooms. Less than half the overhead lights seemed to be working now. Inside the wash-rooms, there were only dim orange emergency lights working, but they gave out just enough light to see what one was doing. Even so, the two women stayed together at all times, fearful of any unforeseen unpleasant eventualities.

They had a little breakfast, Kim barely nibbling a mouse's portion, then packed up again, and drove cautiously out of the bunker.

For a few kilometres, they had to take things very slowly, weaving around any objects on the road that looked as though they could be sharp, and even having to get out of the truck a couple of times to shift large rocks out of the way. Broad drifts of sand lay right across the road in a few places. But then conditions returned to normal, and the tarmac was smooth and unobstructed again. Kim, taking her turn at the wheel, breathed a big sigh of relief, and took the truck up to cruising speed.

The women had settled into a silent companionship, each engrossed in her own thoughts. Kim had been thinking about the long-distant past, and decided to mine Dana's knowledge on the subject.

"So, I know that the world was struck by a really big meteorite, way back, but I've never quite understood much about it, and what happened afterwards. Is that an area that you know much about?"

"Well, it's not my particular period of expertise, but I have studied it, of course. It's an era that is very important for us to study, because it set the scene for who we are as a people nowadays. There is an incredible amount of history prior to the Apocalypse, and it is absolutely fascinating, but it seems quite remote from us now. I'm lucky that I studied under Professor Michael Olinsson at the University, and he's my head of department now. It was always his main area of interest, so I learned quite a lot from him. The Apocalypse was pretty-much a reset for civilisation, and people had to start again from scratch in some ways."

"So, starting from the big event, what do we know now about the meteorite?" asked Kim.

"It is thought now that it was quite a small asteroid, or meteoroid. Still a very large chunk of rock, mark you. It was lucky that it was relatively small, because anything bigger would have probably wiped out nearly all life on earth, rather like the earlier impact which killed off the dinosaurs."

"Yes, I've read about that one."

"Apparently it's virtually impossible to see these things coming. There are some in orbit around the sun, which come round regularly, so they can be plotted, and any on a possible collision course are known about. But this one is thought to have come from outside our solar system, like a rogue one. It was accompanied by a large cluster of other rocks too, which are the ones that visit us each year in the 'season'. Those were added to by the massive explosion resulting from the impact, so that we have even more going around now. Their course got deflected, and the sun's gravity 'adopted' them, so they are now in a new elliptical orbit, at an odd angle from the one Earth travels."

"So what happened when this thing struck?"

"Well, it's thought that its point of impact was a bit unlucky for us. It hit a rift point between two of the earth's tectonic plates, and plunged into a deep well of magma, which meant that it did far more damage than if it had hit a more stable region. A big impact is never good news, mind you. But this was really cataclysmic; the plates are thought to have tilted slightly, causing gigantic tidal waves, and huge amounts of water were projected into space, so that the world has a smaller covering of oceans now. It also set off a chain reaction in volcanoes all around the globe, so that they erupted in a massive way too. The Yellowstone super-volcano in North America was a particularly big example. We also lost a certain amount of the atmosphere, so that our air is a bit thinner than it would have been back then."

"Gosh! It's too frightening to contemplate... How on earth did people survive?"

"Vast numbers didn't survive, of course. Lots of huge coastal cities were obliterated by tsunamis... Then a huge swathe of the planet got smothered in ash and dust. It would have been a really thick coating down where we are now, in tropical and equatorial regions. And it took years to all fall back down to the ground. Decades even, for all of it. So this layer of dust was floating in the upper atmosphere for a long time, like a blanket blotting out the sunlight, and so cooling the world. It actually reversed the global warming that had set in by this point, which was threatening to make the world uninhabitable anyway."

"How do we know about that?"

"Well, the remarkable thing about the Apocalypse, or at least for the people who lived at that time, is that they had electricity, and electronic communications, and recording media. A huge amount of databases in high latitudes survived the impact, and we still have access to them now."

"By 'high latitudes', you mean the areas nearest to the poles, north and south?"

"That's right. There were pockets of survivors who lived in those regions, such as the nordic countries. Communications in fact were largely wiped out by the event, because it fired off a huge electro-magnetic pulse, which cooked a lot of delicate electronic devices.

People already had cellphones at this time, so a lot of them were destroyed by the EMP. Some survived though, if they were shielded in some way from the pulse, but it took a long time for the different pockets of survivors to make contact with each other. Whole comms systems probably went down all at once... Some of the older data recording systems survived better, ironically, because they didn't have electronic circuits at their core; things like laser-etched recorded discs, for example, so we've been able to access huge amounts of information about the world before the Apocalypse."

"But how did the people survive the new conditions, the colder weather, and so on?"

"The people who were most likely to survive, interestingly, were those who already lived in colder climates, such as in nordic countries, who also had the good fortune to be a long way away from the point of impact. They were used to experiencing long dark winters, but they also had the good luck to still have access to hydro-electricity, and nuclear power. It seems that a certain amount of hydro-plants fed by lakes and rivers were largely unaffected by the Apocalypse, so these people still had power! At least until some of the lakes and rivers froze up, anyway. Luckily, engineers had been making preparations for an EMP from a nuclear strike, so they managed to restore the power supplies fairly quickly. It meant that they were able to heat their houses, have lights, and even grow small amounts of crops in glass-houses with artificial lighting. I think that the winters were really brutal, but they survived – just. The ice sheets at the poles extended massively in the early years. But there were a few really clever people who were more far-sighted; there was a guy who was in charge of the botanical gardens in some of the big nordic cities, for instance. He made it his mission to preserve and propagate useful plants which were held in the greenhouses there – things like plants used for pharmaceutical purposes, tea and coffee bushes, and lots of deciduous species, which he feared might have been totally eradicated by the impact's after-effects. That's why we can drink coffee now."

"Incredible!"

"Yes. There was a lot of ingenuity displayed at that time. Desperate times result in desperate measures, I suppose. But things were on a knife-edge for decades. Pockets of people survived, in part, thanks to huge cold stores which held large amounts of food. These were able to keep going because the electricity was still functioning. That kept a lot of people alive for quite a long time. There were also reserves of dried foodstuffs, grain and so on. But we're mainly talking about survivors in small communities. I think that a lot of people in big cities would have run out of food quite early on… It was almost impossible to grow crops for a few years, because there wasn't sufficient light for them to grow to a useful size. But in some places, they were able to have these large glasshouses with artificial lighting, and that saved the day."

"So how long was it before things became more normal again?"

"A very long time. Really, it was survival or subsistence in the early years; but then the light slowly returned, and it became possible to grow crops normally again, after maybe twenty years, when much of the ash fall-out had settled. Another thing I didn't mention was the existence of oil storage tanks in some of the ports. Oil production pretty-much stopped when the asteroid struck, but there was quite a lot of oil in these tanks, and that could keep a small population going for a time. It meant they were able to still catch fish in northern waters. Such fish as survived, that is. But the oil ran out fairly soon, so then they had to quickly develop alternative sources of power – electricity in the main. I think there was a measure of stability by about 100PA (*post-Apocalypse*). But it was *another* hundred years before people could enjoy a more comfortable existence, and not have to concentrate just on surviving. It was a long time before big industries rebuilt themselves."

"It's fascinating. I'm glad that I wasn't living back then though!"

"Too right! Apparently, the population of the world pre-Apocalypse was eight billion, and the event is thought to have killed off 90% of those…"

"Oh, God! That's unthinkable…"

They went quiet for a while, digesting these nightmarish thoughts. Then Kim asked about another aspect to the cataclysm.

"So what happened to governments, and law and order, and organisation? Do we know anything about that?"

"Yes, again, it's quite well documented. Things went rather tribal initially it seems; small communities looking after their own interests. There were survivors among the people in governments of course, and some of them tried reimposing their will and ideas, but that didn't go down too well with lots of the other survivors doing more practical things to eke out an existence! But they had to reorganise themselves, in order to pool resources such as the nuclear power stations, which were so vital to everyone's survival. It's interesting to note that Sweden had actually decided to dismantle all its nuclear power some time before the Apocalypse, but hadn't implemented the decision. That was a bit of luck! Anyway, places like Norway, Sweden and Finland got themselves reorganised relatively quickly. Russia was a bit of a disaster area, because there were too many rival factions, so that tribalism persisted for a long time there. Canada was quite a success story; again, they had a number of nuclear power stations, although some went down as a result of the impact. The greater part of the United States was smothered in ash from the Yellowstone eruption alone, which was catastrophic in every way...

Then in the southern hemisphere, there were large groups of survivors at the southern tip of Africa, where we're going, as well as South America, and a certain amount in southern Australasia. Within a hundred years, there was a new Scandinavian Union, much like we still have nowadays, and it became the dominant and most influential power on earth, with its almost unrivalled technical knowledge and re-emerging industrial base. Fortunately, they had not forgotten about the high standards of social care and human rights which they had developed before the Apocalypse, and these were re-adopted and further developed once life settled down again. Strangely, Scandinavia developed a unique bond with South Africa, thanks to large communities of expatriates who had been living and working in each other's countries. They obviously wanted to re-establish contact with their original homes, and so great efforts were made to rekindle relationships. A great exchange of knowledge and information followed on from that. Canada went its own way, and thrived. Other regions mostly fared rather less well..."

"It's fascinating... So, is most of Africa still uninhabited now?"

"Largely... As we saw earlier on in our trip, there are a few small settlements in the north, where people have migrated from our part of the world, but it's a harsh environment, with finding water a real problem. Then you get into 'meteorite alley', as people call it, and it becomes too dangerous an area to stay in year-round. I suppose it's possible that the meteorites will run out eventually, which would then mean people can colonize some of these areas, but it looks as though it will be a long time before that happens..."

Now and again, they would suddenly roll onto a section of tarmac with a much rougher texture, which would create an unpleasant rasping sound in the truck's cabin, causing them to have to raise their voices a little, or to stay quiet and hope for a smoother stretch to arrive. A rough spell now ended the conversation prematurely.

The landscape was still pancake-flat, with sparse clumps of vegetation, and the occasional distant stump of an old volcanic core, though far smaller than the ones they had seen the previous day. But then, for over an hour, they drove over a section of terrain which became more and more undulating in form. The undulations settled down to an extraordinary regularity, and with an uncomfortably short frequency. It was a real roller-coaster. Both women began to feel nauseous, and were greatly relieved when they came across a parking lay-by. They got out of the truck slowly, grateful for being stationary for a while. The heat was colossal, barely relieved only by the slight breeze. The lay-by was on top of an undulation, so they surveyed the surroundings carefully, and listened for any sound. A vehicle coming from the opposite direction could just suddenly spring into view from a dip, unannounced, in this terrain, which was a bit concerning. But no sound came to their ears; there was nothing within at least ten kilometres of where they stood.

Mercifully, the ground flattened out somewhat fairly soon after they got under way again. Their stomachs settled back down. Dana studied the map on her tablet once again.

"There's another rift, or fault, coming up in about 80km," she announced. "Only this one apparently has a huge change of level. Instead of being a lava river or a chasm, it's like a big cliff-face. I'm not sure how the road gets to the upper level..."

"I can't wait!" answered Kim. "We can be sure it will be something weird again. They don't seem to do normal around these parts!"

"That's true..."

Kim had not been too far out in her prediction. A little under an hour later, the rift came into view. Just as Dana had described, it presented itself as an unending vertical cliff-face, perpendicular to the road, and stretching off into the distance in both directions. As they approached it, they began to understand the scale of the obstacle; it must have been 150 metres from base to upper level. Closer still, their hearts sank when they saw the means by which the road rose up to the higher level.

A huge illuminated sign announced *"Chéchan Fault Helicoidal Leveller. Status: Open"*

Ahead of them, a colossal metallic spiral construction rose up from the lower plain, supported on massive yellow-painted struts with elaborate pointed finials. The cliff face behind it was sheer, bare rock, with a very rough surface, striped along its length by different strata. It was massive and awe-inspiring.

They stopped before driving onto the Leveller, just long enough for Dana to take the wheel again. Kim felt queasy just looking at the great spiral roadway, and was happy to be a passenger again. Dana set off, and they began to climb. It was fine at first, but as they neared the summit, they found it very uncomfortable rounding the part of the loop furthest from the rock face. It felt as though they were just hanging in space, with little to prevent them from plunging groundwards again, despite the solid-looking crash-barriers. The climb only took them seven minutes, but they felt much happier when they reached solid ground again.

They glanced back, taking in the bare cliff-edge stretching away into infinity either way. It was a frightening sight, with the land just seeming to come to an inexplicable edge. Ahead of them, there was a large cafeteria complex on either side of the highway, with numerous parking spaces at forty-five degrees to the kerb. Once again, there seemed to be nobody around. They drove slowly past fast food outlets and trashy souvenir shops, all closed up and dark.

Dana was hoping there would be a recharging station somewhere along here; it seemed inconceivable that there would not be any at such a tourist stop. She felt some relief when she spotted the large sign, with its spark symbol, up ahead on top of a tall metal pole, almost at the end of this forlorn-looking service area. It turned out to be a very civilised place, recently refurbished, with a large canopy to give shade, and rows of parking spots marked out next to each plugging-in point. At the back, there was a sizeable shop which no doubt stocked snacks, ice creams and drinks of all kinds, when it was open. They pulled in, and drove up to the nearest power point. As soon as they had come to a stop, they noticed a hand-written sign taped onto the stand, declaring it to be 'out of order'. They drove on to the next one, and found that it displayed the same message. Moving along slowly, they inspected all twelve power points. Only the very last one did not show a sign. They got out of the truck, and Dana did the business with the cable and her payment card. It seemed to be working, and they breathed another big sigh of relief. It could have presented a problem if they had been unable to recharge here, even with the portable cells they were carrying. Dana realised that she was leaving an electronic trail with the recharging transactions, but it couldn't be helped. She doubted that anyone would drive hundreds of kilometres to investigate. There was the risk that police would use the evidence to slap a 5000 kroner fine on them, for driving in a prohibited area during meteorite season, but she couldn't worry about that. There were more important issues at stake here.

The truck drank up its charge, and the two women stretched their legs, ambling slowly around in the shade of the overhead canopy, keeping a weather ear open for any sound of another vehicle. They dared not go further than twenty or thirty metres away from the truck. They watched large lizards scuttle across the forecourt around them, heading for raised sunny spots in which to recharge their own batteries. A particularly big example gave chase to another one, and fought it briefly, before the smaller one rushed off at great speed. They asked one another light-heartedly whether it was any kind of omen, but decided not to have such foolish thoughts.

After twenty minutes, the truck's instrument screen showed that it had 80% of its huge potential charge. They were anxious to get going again; the remaining 20% would take much longer to go in, and so they set off again. The buildings petered out, and they found themselves in open terrain once more, but 150 metres higher than before their spiral ascent of the Leveller. It looked no different to the lower level at first, but soon the ground developed a gentle, and quite pleasant, long undulating nature. However, they could see one or two small meteorite impact craters in the distance on either side.

Suddenly, they could make out the tall rim of a large crater directly ahead of them, in a slight depression in the land. It gradually became clearer, until the point when they realised that this crater had resulted from a direct hit on the H2 highway. As they got closer, they could see that a section of the tarmac surface of the road had been heaved up, so that it formed an abrupt ramp canted upwards at 45 degrees to the ground. They slowed down as they approached the massive obstruction, shocked by the scale of it, and by the freshness of its appearance. The rim was all newly-formed, bare sandy soil, with no trace of new growth of any kind on its surface. A little wisp of smoke rose from inside the crater.

"Oh my God," cried Kim; "how are we going to get past this?"

"Wait a minute," replied Dana, "someone's been here before us - look!"

She pointed to a set of tyre tracks heading off the road to the left of the crater, and appearing to go around the obstruction. They stopped and got out of the truck, and walked along the tracks a short distance. Then Dana clambered up the slope of the rim to get a higher perspective on the area, and Kim joined her soon after. They could see quite a long way from up here.

"It doesn't look too difficult" said Dana. "I think maybe a couple of cars have been here before us; it's reasonably flat, and the truck is supposed to be able to handle rough ground. Let's give it a try."

"I suppose that, in about a month's time, the road will have been diverted around this thing," observed Kim. "But right now, there's a delay in repair work…"

Addendum

Please add extra pages where marked *
on page 65

SIX

Fifty kilometres on, they were driving through a wide open area. The road would take an occasional slight change of direction, but generally it took the form of very long, dead straight stretches, heading more or less due south, sometimes diving into a dip for a few kilometres before rising again. Low hills formed a long line over to the east. The two women had gone quiet, each lost in her own thoughts, scanning the landscape surrounding them, and peering into the far distance to anticipate any potential problem ahead. Kim was driving, when Dana suddenly caught the briefest glimpse of another vehicle, a long way ahead of them.

"There's something up ahead," she said simply. They peered carefully into the hazy distance, trying to ascertain which way the other vehicle was travelling.

"There it is!" said Kim, spotting the car that was far away, but which seemed to be growing bigger. "It's coming this way..."

"Oh, no... You're right. OK, we'll see who it is. Maybe they'll just race past, like before."

They slowed just a little, keeping their eyes glued on the place where the road faded into nothing. The heat haze came and went slightly, and suddenly, they saw the other vehicle much more clearly, approaching fast. It was a car, with some kind of object or bar fixed to its roof.

"I don't believe it... it's a cop car..." said Dana. "Why would they even be here?"

As they watched, the police car's blue flashing lights lit up on the roof, and it stopped in the middle of the highway, on a diagonal, so that it took up most of the road's width. There was no possibility of ignoring it. A couple of minutes later, Kim was slowing to a halt just short of the cop car.

Dana and Kim got out of the truck at almost the same moment as the two policemen climbed out of their car. They waited for the cops to come across to them, sizing them up as they walked their way. The two men were similar to each other in age, probably in their late thirties, and looked surprisingly smart and well-groomed, but not over-friendly in demeanour.

"Good morning," said one of the cops. "Would you like to tell us what brings you out here?"

"We're heading for Mandela, officer," said Dana.

"And where from, exactly? You don't appear to be from these parts," the guy replied, gesturing towards the truck's obvious northern number-plate. "Can we see your I.D. please?"

"I'll get it," said Kim, going back to the truck, and locating their driving licences and identity cards in the glove box. She handed the documents over to the lead cop.

"So... You have come from Laxberg, in meteorite season, which as you must be well aware, is forbidden. Why are you heading for Mandela?"

Dana explained the reasons for their epic journey, and their anxiety over the fate of their husbands, and emphasised how well-prepared they were for the long trip.

"That is beside the point, said the lead cop. I am sure that if you had just waited, the news would have come to you sooner or later. But you have deliberately ignored the law, and ventured across dangerous territory to make this unnecessary journey!"

"It didn't seem unnecessary to us..." said Kim. "We've been continually fobbed off by officialdom, and we just want to find out what's happened to our husbands. We're not causing anyone any trouble here."

"And what would happen if everyone decided to do like you? The roads would be full of traffic, and lots of people would be dying in meteorite strikes! There's a reason for the road closure – it's to protect foolish people like you!"

"We've encountered no particular problems..." answered Dana, bending the truth very slightly.

"You've just been very fortunate!" said the cop. "We can't have people just taking the law into their own hands. We're going to issue you with a 5,000 Kroner fine each, and send you on your way."

"Each?" squeaked Kim. "Surely you don't have to be so harsh?"

"We can't have people just ignoring the law! Maybe this will make you two think harder about your actions in future."

"Oh, for God's sake!" cried Dana. "This is just so unreasonable..."

"Nonsense! This is the law, and you deliberately chose to ignore it. There will be no discussion here."

The two cops began to fill out the official paperwork for the fines, while Dana and Kim stood quietly seething with resentment, gazing at the landscape around them without seeing anything. Tears began to come to Kim's eyes, but she turned away and wiped them away casually, not wanting to show any sign of weakness. The cops finished their form-filling, and handed over the women's portions.

"There you are," said the lead cop. "You have 28 days to settle the fines, or else to lodge an appeal. There is very little history of success in that direction, I should advise you. Now, you will turn around, and return to where you started from. Good day."

"What?" exclaimed Dana. "You want us to turn around and go back? But we're much closer to Mandela now – only about three days' driving!"

"That's no concern of ours... In any case, the road is blocked further south, so you won't get through."

"I don't believe this!" said Kim. "You can be sure that we'll issue a complaint about you two. We have your badge numbers."

"I can assure you that you will not get any sympathy from the authorities. It's quite clear-cut. Now, on your way please!"

The two cops stood in the road, watching, as Dana and Kim returned slowly to their truck and climbed back in. Kim fastened her seat-belt with trembling hands, started the motor, and began to execute a three-point turn. The two of them felt a mixture of anger and despair. Kim set off again, heading in the wrong direction.

"Those bloody bastards!" cried Dana. "Smug shits... I've never wanted more to kick a guy in the groin!"

"That might not have helped our case..." observed Kim. "But I don't know why they had to be so vindictive... Now, let's calm down a bit here. What are we going to do? We can't just drive all the way back home again... I'm just not doing it. Look back, Dana. What are those pricks doing? Are they following us, or are they turning around?"

Dana peered round, trying to look through the small back window of the truck, and also looking in the wing mirror, although that made everything look smaller.

"I think they're turning round. Let's just go a little way, stop, and try to work out what we can do. I'm damned if I'm going to be sent back when we're so close to Mandela..."

They drove for about ten kilometres, then stopped at the roadside, and looked at the maps on their tablets, trying to work out if there was an alternative route to the H2.

"There's a parallel road, some distance away, maybe fifty kilometres to the east," said Dana after a while. "It's not that big, needless to say. And I think there's a small road off this one which joins up with it, about twenty kilometres north of here. It might not be much more than a track, that's the only worry. I can't say that I've really noticed any proper side-turnings..."

"Hmmm... Well, it's worth a try. But will we recognise this turning when we get to it?"

"I'm not certain. We're not getting a very accurate fix on our position, because of the solar flare activity, so if it's not very obvious, then we might just sail past it..."

"Well, we've got plenty of time. We'll just keep going back and forth until we find it, if we have to!"

"Yes, good. Slow down in about ten to fifteen minutes, and we'll keep our eyes skinned."

They moved off again, and slowed right down to a crawl about fifteen kilometres further north, inspecting the land to the east very closely.

"This could be it!" said Dana, staring at a track which seemed to lead off, perpendicular to the main highway.

Kim brought the truck to a halt alongside the beginning of the side turning. There was no sign to indicate any destination, and the verge of the main road looked singularly unmarked by vehicles which might have turned off in recent times. Nevertheless, they decided to try their luck, and Kim turned slowly off the smooth highway. The surface was not as bad as Dana had feared. There was tarmac present, but this had become grown over in large areas by grass and other plants, especially along its centre-line. Where the tarmac survived, it had a coarse, granular appearance, as well as some cracking. Even so, it was definitely a route of some kind, leading somewhere... Kim felt the weight of responsibility of driving on this rough road, with the potential of damage to the truck.

"Are you OK with me driving, Dana? Or do you want to take over? It's your truck after all..."

"I'm fine, Kim. You're doing great. Just take it steady like this, and we shouldn't have a problem. It's not like it's full of pot-holes or anything..."

"Not so far, no..."

They carried on carefully. Dana looked back towards the main highway, checking to see if the cops might have followed them after all, but there was nothing and nobody to be seen. She turned back and looked ahead. The landscape they were going through was fairly featureless sparse grassland, punctuated here and there with a stunted shrub and the odd succulent type of plant with broad spiky leaves. The road dropped into a broad dip, on the far side of which it climbed again, turning slightly to the left. They would be invisible from the main H2 by now, so they breathed a little more easily for the moment. They felt anxious about what might lie further ahead though, and whether there was any chance of their bumping into the cops again further south. But they decided to try and take one step at a time, and plead ignorance if challenged.

"How far have we come since turning off the H2?" asked Dana.

""About sixteen kilometres now," replied Kim. "So, thirty-four to go, roughly, is that right?"

"Yes, something like that..."

They kept going steadily, watching out carefully for any potentially hazardous holes or stray rocks on the track. So far, so good. The roadway meandered slightly, but kept generally heading eastwards. They should find the southbound road before too long. From what they could make out from the map, it looked as though it should be a reasonably good road, if not a major highway like the H2. It might even have been the original main road south, before the H2 was constructed on a more direct line.

Thirty-five minutes later, they could see the main road up ahead, disappearing into the distance left and right. After another five minutes, Kim was very carefully steering the truck over the lumpy verge of the main road, and turning right, to head southwards once again.

"Great! Well done Kim. Would you like a rest now? I'll take the wheel again if you like."

"Yes, thanks. That would be good. I'd like to just run up and down a bit too, and burn off some of the adrenaline..."

"OK. Let's both do that."

They stopped and got out of the truck, and spent five minutes doing some vigorous exercise. It was a bit hot for such activity, but they would cool down soon enough with the truck's air-con. They sat back down, and turned up the fan speed, while poring over the map to check the route ahead.

"It seems straightforward enough," said Dana. "It might not be quite as straight and smooth as the H2, but it's going the right way, and we can rejoin the main highway further south if we want."

"Not too soon, I think. I don't want to bump into those two shits again!"

"No... I'm just not sure where they might be based... Are they patrolling up and down, or what?"

"Hard to say... I'm tempted to think that we should try and outrun them if we see them again, but I don't know if that's realistic?"

"Probably not. This thing wouldn't be as fast as their cop car... But look, I think the likelihood of our coming across them again is very low. Let's stay on this road for the time being. With luck, the cops stick to the H2."

They resumed their southward journey. They had wasted over two hours by having to divert to this parallel route, but although this was frustrating, it was not a huge amount in terms of the overall journey. Aside from the damaged wheel, they had been fairly lucky until the encounter with the officious cops. If there was no further mishap, they could not complain too much.

Although this smaller road was less straight than the H2, it proved to have a good enough surface, and so they were able to resume their previous cruising speed. The road took a slightly more scenic route, following the ridge of a line of low hills for a time, and winding left and right as it went, before dropping back into the seemingly endless plain. After ninety minutes or so, they realised when they consulted the map that the lesser road was gradually converging back towards the H2, and would hit it after another hundred and fifty kilometres. They would then have to make the decision on whether to take another detour on a minor road, or take their chances with cops on the main H2. When the time came, they found that their patience was wearing thin, and they decided to live dangerously, rejoining the major highway that led to Mandela. They decided to try and keep their vehicle well hidden during overnight stops, and to try their utmost to hide if they should spot any other vehicle in the distance.

***

They returned to the truck, and headed for the edge of the tarmac, following the tracks of the vehicles which had preceded them. They soon discovered that what looked smooth from a slight elevation was surprisingly bumpy. The truck pitched and heaved like a boat in a storm, so Dana took it very slowly and carefully. Some sections smoothed out considerably, but then there would be another big hollow or rock to negotiate. Nevertheless, after fifteen minutes, they had circumnavigated the great obstruction, and they climbed back onto smooth tarmac. They had to take it carefully for a couple of hundred metres, because rocks and sand were strewn haphazardly over the highway, but then the way was clear again for them.

They pressed on, greatly relieved to have surmounted this obstacle relatively easily, but slightly concerned that there might be more such problems ahead. The journey was quite long enough without such delays occurring every few hours... From time to time, one or other of them would grow worried about the scale of what they had embarked upon, and how incredibly far they were from home, and from any kind of help if something should go wrong. This, together with their anxiety over the fate of their menfolk, would result in some quiet, introspective spells, during which they felt close to being overwhelmed by the situation. The women could barely express the solace they both felt at having each other's company and moral support.

They drove on a further 250 kilometres before stopping again briefly to stretch their legs. They both tried their cellphones once more. There was still no word from Garth or Calum, but then communications were almost non-existent. The news channels just carried indecipherable paragraphs of garbled words, and no pictures at all; while this was a slight improvement on the earlier state of affairs, it was of no use whatsoever.

"What on earth do you think has happened to them?" asked Kim. "And why do we still have this comms problem?"

"I don't know, Kim. I keep trying to figure it out, and I've been trying to remember what happened in previous years at the end of the meteorite season, and I don't remember particularly. I suppose I had

no real reason to take much notice before... Did Calum ever travel down south before?"

Kim thought for a minute before answering.

"Yes, he's had to work near Mandela before, but usually out of the meteorite season. He was down there during the season two years ago, I think. We couldn't talk for about four weeks because of the comms interference, but then it came back, and he was able to travel home soon after."

"Did he fly?"

"Oh, yes, it takes far too long to go by road - as we're discovering! But of course, you have to have a pretty good reason to go by air."

"Yes, I know; Garth has flown down there too, but I've never even been up in an aircraft..."

"Never? I flew once, a few years ago. It was amazing! A bit scary though..." said Kim.

Flying was generally the preserve of government officials or vital employees, because aircraft needed large quantities of hydrogen, which took huge amounts of power to generate. Mass air travel had never become a realistic possibility after the apocalypse, due to this problem, which was exacerbated by the slightly thinner atmosphere. The use of fossil fuels had been prohibited by law many years earlier, so hydrogen had to be produced by using renewable energy.

"I feel sure that they are OK," Dana said, in an attempt to sound reassuring. "I'm sure I would know it if something had happened to Garth. Sometimes I feel that it's almost like we're one person!"

"Yes, I often feel that way too, but I can't help worrying... If only we could understand what's happening..." Tears came to Kim's eyes, and she shuddered a couple of times, desperately trying to regain her composure. Dana put her arms around her and hugged her, feeling relief at having this comforting physical contact, and knowing that she was not alone in having these fears. They both shed a few tears, then made a great effort, and pulled themselves together.

They set off again. The terrain was becoming more rugged, with dry valleys, hills, and low rocky escarpments carved out of the land here and there. Dana noticed on her map that they were approaching a place called the Devil's Fingers. She vaguely recalled hearing about this; it was supposed to be a series of rock needles jutting skywards, from what she could remember.

They saw the needles from a long way away, but had slight difficulty interpreting the scale, in the slight heat haze which hung in the distant landscape. It seemed to take a long time to reach them, but as they grew closer, and the air cleared, low stubby rock formations prodded upwards with increasing frequency to their right, and these gradually morphed into gigantic needles towering up towards the sky. The ones closest to the highway canted over at forty-five degrees, and jutted right across the gently curving path of the road, hanging over it in an extraordinarily threatening manner. The tips of two of the needles had broken off, and enormous sections of rock lay either side of the highway. Huge triangular signs warned of falling rocks, and the two women wondered whether these served any useful purpose at all, other than inducing terror into the hearts of passing travellers.

The Devil's Fingers were yet another awesome spectacle, but they did not feel comfortable lingering below the overhanging sections; they sped beneath them, and stopped at the far end to gaze back in wonder for a few minutes, while having a much-needed drink.

All was silent around them, and the sky was beginning to take on a pinky hue low down. They would soon need to find a place to spend the night. They drove on a bit further, their eyes constantly scanning the surroundings for a suitable hiding place. The rocky terrain offered a few possibilities, but they settled on a spot just off the road, in a kind of shallow cave formed by a slightly overhanging section of rock. It was situated on the eastern side of the road, so that the morning sun would not spotlight their presence to anyone who might pass by. They still felt wary of any other road users, and preferred not having to explain their presence to any officialdom. They hoped that they would just merge unobserved into other traffic once they got near to their destination.

SIX

The night passed without any drama, but the morning revealed a number of large ants and scorpions scurrying about their otherwise perfect camp-site. They walked cautiously around the truck, eyes cast downwards to avoid treading on any of the local inhabitants. When they were ready to leave, they sat sideways in their seats, and banged their feet together before swinging their legs into the truck, hoping to dislodge any ants which might be clinging to their shoes. They rejoined the highway with some relief.

"It's hard to imagine now, that this area was teeming with big animals before the Apocalypse..." observed Dana.

"Yes, I know," replied Kim.

"Have you seen the archive footage at the Natural History Museum in Laxberg?"

"No - dating from when?" asked Kim.

"It's real video footage, pre-Apocalypse. It's a temporary exhibition which started about a month ago. There's a special little auditorium where they play these ancient things. As I was saying yesterday, they've been able to copy the original footage from discs or whatever onto modern formats, and so preserve them for ever. They're mind-blowing - this place would have been vast grass-lands way back then, full of deer, giraffes, lions and leopards. Elephants too."

"It must have been amazing! The world has lost so much... But then, from what you were saying, there were even bigger extinction events before, like when the dinosaurs were wiped out.."

"Oh yes... In reality, mankind got a bit lucky with the scale of the last one. But it probably didn't feel like it at the time! As you said, I'm glad we're living now, rather than 2,000 years ago..."

"Yes. It must have been an absolutely terrifying time..."

They charged on, and for an hour or so played some rousing music on the truck's sound system, singing along to stirring choruses, and quietly enjoying delicate instrumental passages and intricate guitar solos. They compared memories of wonderful festivals they had attended when they were a little younger.

They stopped mid-morning, to stretch their legs a bit, and have a pee. There was some sparse vegetation around; clumps of quite tall grasses, and large aloes. Having looked into the far distance to ascertain that no other vehicles were approaching, the women crouched behind plants. Kim was suddenly startled by the sound of Dana shrieking loudly a couple of times, and looked up to see her friend hopping back towards the truck.

"Oh hell! Something's bitten me! And now I've twisted my ankle trying to get away from it... Oh, you stupid, stupid, stupid mare!" Dana remonstrated with herself.

"It's OK! Let me take a look," said Kim, immediately adopting her calm paramedic's manner. "Where's the bite, and did you see what bit you?"

"It was a beetle of some kind; it just suddenly landed on my hand. It might have fallen off one of those plants where I was. Shit! It hurts... And then, just to help matters, I twisted my ankle in my rush to get away from the stupid thing! Oh, hell..."

"OK. It's probably nothing to worry about too much. I'll just get my first aid kit from the back, and put something on it. Can you sit on the seat here," she said, motioning Dana to sit sideways in the back of the truck. She found her medical kit , which she had put together using her expert knowledge; it contained far more than most people's domestic sets. "What kind of a bug was it?"

"It was a multi-coloured beetle, with a long thin body; quite big..."

"Right," she said; "I'm not really sure whether that needs a specific antidote; it's not that likely, so I'll wash it carefully, then apply a topical steroid cream. I might give you some antibiotics for a few days too. I'll look at your ankle afterwards."

"Oh, Kim! I'm so sorry..."

"Don't be so silly... It could have happened to me just as easily. It's only a little thing – you haven't broken anything, have you?"

"No, I don't think so, though it's pretty sore. But I'm worried that I might not be able to drive... Oh, hell, what are we going to do?"

"What we're going to do is not panic, Dana! I can still drive, and I expect you'll be all right by morning. Now, hold still and let me deal with your hand."

Kim examined Dana's left hand. The back of it was already looking quite red and swollen. She washed it with soap and water, rinsed that away, then applied a liberal blob of steroid cream. Then she covered it loosely with a gauze bandage.

"OK?" she asked.

"Yes," Dana replied, slightly unconvincingly.

Kim then gently peeled Dana's shoe and sock off, and examined the ankle, very gently manipulating it this way and that. Dana winced, but did not yell.

"I think it's just a sprain," said Kim. I'll bind it, and then perhaps you could leave your shoe off for now. I'll drive, and we'll see how it is later on. It might swell up."

"All right, thank you very much."

Kim did the business, then helped Dana get in to the front passenger seat of the truck. She put her medical kit on the back seat, and got behind the wheel to set off again. Dana closed her eyes, and dozed off after a little while, but woke up again with a start after only twenty minutes.

"How does it feel?" Kim asked.

"It's not bad; it feels a bit hot maybe..."

"That's not unexpected. I think I will give you that antibiotic when we next stop though, and some antihistamines too..." Beneath her calm demeanour, Kim felt more than a little concerned, although she was not going to let that show. She had heard some real horror stories about insect bites in such wild places. But what more could she do? She secretly began fretting again about the impetuous folly of this journey. Why had they not just stayed at home and waited for news, like good obedient citizens? She took a deep breath, and tried to put these thoughts out of her mind, and turned her attention to the landscape they were passing through.

The surrounding terrain had flattened out again, and they were passing through an area covered in stones of all sizes. There were still clumps of grass, and a scattering of smooth-leaved cactus-like plants. More ominously, there were still impact craters dotting the landscape, though they were more spaced out than in earlier areas. Of course, some of them were undoubtedly ancient. A breeze had got up, and the sandy ground between stones and plants had taken on a rippled appearance, like on a beach at low tide.

Two hours later, the wind had become strong and blustery, and they could feel it buffeting the truck. The terrain had become increasingly sandy, and the sky had taken on a milky white colour, with a tinge of brown. It looked like the beginnings of a real dust storm. The air all around them had acquired thickness, or so it seemed, and visibility was becoming increasingly difficult. They seemed to be passing through a sandy desert area now, with sand dunes rolling away into the distance, or at least, as far as they could see. In some stretches, the course of the road became tricky to decipher, because great drifts of sand had blown across the tarmac, obliterating the black-top for 100 metres at a time. Kim felt decidedly uneasy about this new hazard thrown their way, but said nothing. Dana was the first to voice her fears.

"Oh hell! I really don't like this Kim... Can you make out the road OK? What happens if we accidentally drive off the tarmac? We could be stuck here until someone finds us!"

"Stay calm girl... I can still see where we're going – just! We'll just take it very carefully. We must keep moving..."

It struck Kim that Dana's normally self-possessed nature seemed to have deserted her since the earlier incident. More than ever before, she needed to stay in control here, and keep the both of them calm. Kim had had to slow down considerably for safety's sake, and was concentrating extra hard to pick out the way ahead. She kept going however, because this would have been an impossibly inhospitable place to stop. She hoped against hope that conditions would improve, and kept wondering about how the highway was kept clear in normal times. Would they use a kind of snow-plough device to shift the sand?

Dana had gone very quiet, occasionally closing her eyes for a bit. A gruelling forty minutes later, she suddenly seemed to wake from her torpor and became animated.

"Oh, Kim! I think I recognise this place. Look, I think that if you pull in over there, we can go to the water's edge, and there's a kiosk selling ice creams..."

Kim looked round at her companion, who was gazing into the distance absent-mindedly. She suddenly noticed that there was a sheen of perspiration on Dana's forehead, and her pupils looked quite dilated. She realised that Dana had developed a fever, and was becoming delirious. She could feel her own anxiety levels rising, but was determined to remain calm, and adopted her best paramedic poker-face.

"No, we can't get out of the car here Dana, we're in a sandstorm! Now listen to me – we're going to stop just for a minute, so I can give you an antibiotic. OK? But we're not getting out of the truck! It's too dangerous..."

"OK, Kim."

"Do you feel hot?" asked Kim.

"Yeah, I'm absolutely boiling... I think I'll just open the window for a bit to get some air..."

"NO DANA! Don't touch it! The cab will fill up with sand! Let's direct the fan onto your face to cool you a bit."

Kim adjusted the air-con settings, then stopped the truck, and pressed the door locking button in case Dana suddenly decided to go exploring. She reached over to the back seat for her first-aid kit, and looked through its contents. Ciproactinoformicin - that was the one! The new, strongest antibiotic in the world, developed from antibiotics made by ants. She wasn't going to mess about here; she would harness the power of one insect to combat the venom of another one, at the same time as killing any infection. She had heard good reports about its efficacy.

"Right, Dana, take a couple of these. I'll give you these antihistamines as well, and a couple of acetaminophen to reduce your fever. You'll be fine soon."

"Oh, I like those blue ones - what a pretty colour they are! Thank you so much, Kim..."

"They might not taste so good if you suck them, so swallow them straight down."

"All right."

They both took a good swig of water, then Kim set off again into the maelstrom of sand and dust. Dana settled back in her seat, a glazed expression on her face, and dozed intermittently. Kim was glad to not have any distraction while she concentrated on picking out the course of the road between the swathes of yellow-grey dirt. How she hated these conditions... The dust-filled sky seemed to have closed right in on them, leaving nothing for the eye to focus on, other than narrow strips of dusty tarmac here and there.

Some time later, as they continued crawling southwards, Kim dared to begin thinking that perhaps the wind-speed was decreasing. She wondered whether maybe the storm was heading north, so that they had just clipped one edge of it, and were now moving out of it again. The drifts of sand across the road gradually became smaller, and visibility slowly improved. The two women's spirits lifted and their confidence grew; feeling a strange sense of elation, they began to make silly jokes about vehicles being stuck in sand-drifts.

Kim had driven the whole day so far, because they had not dared stop and open the doors recently, for fear of the inside of the truck filling with sand. Enough had blown in through the air vents as it was, despite their having virtually closed up the intake of air. But now they stopped for a rest, and for Dana to take the next dose of antibiotics. There was just the occasional little sand-laden gust of breeze, but nothing to worry about. Kim jogged up and down the edge of the road a little, trying to restore circulation and generate endorphins; it was good to get slightly out of puff. Dana seemed a bit more lively, and less hot; she swung her legs out through the open door, and bent them and stretched them repeatedly. They enjoyed a long draught of water and a little sweet treat, and Kim took the wheel again.

Towards late afternoon, they began to see what looked like large buildings ahead of them. It made no sense, as they were sure that they were a huge distance from any civilisation. But as they came nearer, they realised that these were not man-made structures, but rock formations jutting out of the ground. Many of them had quite a rectangular shape, so that they looked very much like buildings from a quick glance. But when they passed close to some of the formations, they could see that they were formed of eroded sandstone, sculpted over millennia by the wind and sand. The rocks continued for kilometre after kilometre; it looked as though they would never end. But the area also became more and more enchanting in appearance, with more flora finding root in the increasingly sheltered conditions provided by the rocks. Various woody plants and stunted trees could be seen, including drought-tolerant varieties of olive, cypress, mastic trees and oleander. The women decided that they would be wise to find a safe overnight stopping place in this area; it should be relatively easy to locate a spot that was well hidden from the road. Better to stop in a safe place and set off early, than to keep going and find themselves in wide open country again.

They found the perfect place, out of sight of any possible passing vehicle, and benefiting from the last of the day's weakish sunlight.

They were able to enjoy a delightful evening, among the rocks, admiring the flora, and feeling the warmth radiating from the rock faces. It was an unexpectedly pleasant end to the day, after the earlier threat of the sand-storm, and Dana's mishap. The sun set quite early in these latitudes, so they took advantage of the fact to get an early night.

SEVEN

It was such a relief that everything had worked out so well in the end. Kim felt the greatest contentment and fulfilment of her entire life. It was so wonderful to be enjoying this blissful beach holiday together, just the three of them. The temperature was wonderfully warm, and the sea was balmy too. She was treading water, just out of her depth, but close enough to the shore to be able to look back and gaze in love and wonder at Calum, holding their gorgeous baby daughter, happily sleeping in a sling against his chest. He looked fit and tanned, and was standing on the sand with another young dad with a young child, the three of them talking animatedly and laughing. The little girl standing with the other dad was looking up at the two men, giving her opinions now and then, laughing too.

Kim swam a few strokes parallel to the shore, watching small fish scuttling below her. She turned back to face the shore, but the others had all disappeared. Where could they have vanished to so suddenly? A cold panic gripped her stomach, and she started to head back for the beach, but could not seem to make any progress. There were loud warning cries behind her, and she turned around to look. The waves had suddenly grown much bigger, their frothy tops breaking with a hiss. The sky had turned a dark grey, and a huge tornado was bearing down on her, sucking up the seawater and fish, and sending them flying in a great spiral which disappeared upwards. She turned back to the shore, and shouted with all her might:

"Calum, Calum, help me!" He was there again, looking at her, eyes wide in horror, but seemed rooted to the spot.

"Calum, help me!"

"Kim, wake up, wake up! It's all right, you're safe, it's just a dream!"

She woke up, gasping for breath, totally disorientated. She was in the back of the truck; Dana was leaning over her, holding her wrists.

"Oh Dana! Oh God, I'm sorry, I was having a nightmare..."

"It's OK, nothing's happened, you're all right..."

"Yes... Oh, hell, it was so real... There was a tornado... I'd had my baby... But, wait a minute, what about you? You were so unwell last night... Has your fever gone?"

"I seem to be all right, amazingly! I don't feel hot at all."

"Oh, thank goodness for that! I was really worried about you. I'll look at your hand in a minute."

It took Kim some time to recover from the nightmare. She was very quiet for half an hour or more, processing the memory of it, wondering if it could be a premonition of some kind. Logic told her this was nonsense, but the images in the dream had looked so real... Dana could see that it had affected her, and tried hard to jolly her out of her trance-like state. After they had had some breakfast, she began to seem like her old self again, and the two of them pored over the maps on their tablets, trying to establish where they would be travelling through in the coming day.

They unwound the bandage from Dana's hand, and Kim examined it carefully. It was looking slightly improved, although there was still redness and swelling. But Dana had managed to sleep reasonably well, and the hand was not giving her much pain. Kim gave her another dose of the antibiotics to be safe, and applied more steroid cream. The ankle, on the other hand, seemed little better. She would not be driving for a while yet.

It was cool in the shadow cast by the great rock they had parked alongside, and so they moved out into the sunlight, Dana hobbling slowly, and enjoyed a last look at the unusual trees and shrubs here, while trying to keep clear of any insect life on their branches. It was a totally different environment from anything they had seen before.

They set off before very long, not wishing to linger too long when there was still so far to travel. The air had become still again, the sky was perfectly clear, and the day promised to become quite hot once more. After an hour's driving, the sandstone rock formations slowly became smaller and more spaced apart, and the landscape grew more rolling in form. The number of trees and shrubs declined too, with just grasses and stunted, parched-looking aloes peppering the ground thinly.

***

They continued chatting sporadically, while drinking in the sights of the rugged landscape. Kim felt greatly relieved to have the old Dana back again. Fifty kilometres further on, the road dived abruptly down into a deep dry rift. There had been some information signs about this, but the reality of it still took them by surprise. They found themselves travelling down a seemingly never-ending steep slope, while the rock faces on either side became ever higher, feeling as though they were plunging towards the centre of the earth. The truck careered down the hillside, hauled downward by the almost irresistible pull of gravity. The light slowly decreased as the sky gradually became a narrow blue band up above, and the whining sound of the truck's motor and the swishing of the tyres echoed off the hard rock around them. It felt frighteningly unnatural, but the smooth tarmac surface reassured them that this was a bona-fide highway.

After the heat above, it was deliciously cool within the rift, which snaked very slightly this way and that, but generally kept a south-easterly course once it had flattened out. It was surprisingly dark, so that the truck's lights had come on automatically. Dana felt really uneasy in the enclosed space, with the lit-up vehicle shouting out "look at me!" She dreaded the idea of meeting someone else down here; there was no place whatsoever to hide... The rock faces on either side towered above them, marked by different-coloured strata, which sometimes sloped at unexpected angles from the horizontal. There were a few slightly wider portions, which had allowed the creation of parking areas, but they ignored these. They imagined that these places would be very unpleasant to stop in during normal times, with the abominable racket of countless vehicles impossible to get away from. They both felt decidedly claustrophobic in this sinister place, and hurried on towards the point at which the highway returned to the surface, thirty kilometres further on.

They both sighed with relief, which made them chuckle at each other, when they resurfaced into the overpowering daylight. The landscape had changed slightly while they were in the rift; there seemed to be more plants and stubby fat trees, quiver trees maybe, and it all looked greener. To their great delight, they even noticed small areas covered in a colourful carpet of wildflowers. There must have been a bit of rain here recently. In the distance ahead, a purplish line of low mountains beckoned.

"I think we're getting somewhere at last!" said Dana. We've got about another two days of driving to go after those mountains, and then we'll be near Mandela!"

"Oh, thank God for that!" cried Kim. "Your truck is very comfortable, but I'm getting cramp in my backside from sitting for days!" They giggled at this for a couple of minutes; it was good to have little things like this to release the tension they both felt.

***

"You were telling me about life after the Apocalypse the other day," said Kim, "but do we know anything about how people reacted to event, what they initially thought had happened, and whether it had an effect on them spiritually?"

"That's a very interesting aspect to the whole thing of course, and with long-lasting repercussions..." began Dana. "The impact was so massive that the explosion was heard more than 2,500 miles away, and the entire world shook! People immediately had all kinds of thoughts; many assumed that there had been an explosion quite near to them, naturally, because there was no way of telling it had happened so far away. There were those who thought that some military or chemical facility had exploded, while others assumed that there had been a strike with nuclear weapons. The world's super-powers, the United States, Russia, and China, had each built up enormous stocks of nuclear weapons, and there had been fears of nuclear wars for decades before the Apocalypse. Other, smaller countries had these things too, and there were worries about small rogue states getting hold of them to take out their perceived enemies for religious and ideological reasons or whatever. It had grown into an appalling situation. The notion that there had been a tit-for-tat nuclear strike persisted for some time, partly because many people had heard of the electro-magnetic pulse effect.

So what you had was groups of survivors in the most remote areas, unable to obtain news for a long time, and assuming that scenario. At first, things didn't look too different to them; it was just a news and communications black-out. The skies looked normal. But after a few days, the sky began going dark with the ash and dust, as it spread around the whole globe. For many, that was a confirmation of the nuclear war theory, since they had also read about 'nuclear winter.' Then the dust began slowly falling to the ground, over a very long period. Slightly less so towards the poles, mind you. So people assumed that they would contract radiation sickness, since they could not get away from this dust. It was only some weeks later, when they realised that they weren't going down with the sickness, that they turned to other hypotheses. Gradually, the news filtered down that there had been this massive impact from an extra-terrestrial body, and that the dark skies would be staying for a long time... Meanwhile, it was getting colder and colder, because the sun's light wasn't penetrating through to the ground.

Of course, some radical religious groups began putting out the idea that this was a punishment sent by God, and that everyone should spend their days praying for forgiveness for their sins. That didn't sit too well with more practical types, and those who couldn't see what sins babies and small children had committed, not to mention all the various animals. And all the while, as I was saying before, you had some heroic types who ensured that power supplies were restored or continued, or took practical steps to make sure that food could be accessed, for the good of everyone.

In Scandinavia, there was a pragmatic approach to these practical problems; communications slowly improved between all the little communities, until the point arrived when groups met to discuss the possibility of a future, and governments reorganised themselves, and discussed options with the population. The consensus gradually emerged, for the survivors anyway, that perhaps this event could be seen as a new opportunity; a new start. Mankind had raped the earth from the time of the Industrial Revolution, burned fossil fuels in astronomical quantities, and set in train an apparently unstoppable global warming process, which was beginning to look as though it would wipe out most of humanity. So here was the earth suddenly cooling down again. If this could be survived – a big 'if'! - then here was the chance to begin again in an ecologically sustainable way. Scandinavia had a good record for supporting the more vulnerable members of society, and valuing care for the elderly and infirm. They felt that this was a model worth retaining, even though it would be difficult while everyone was in 'survival mode.' But most people agreed that values and ideals needed to be modified a little. Consumerism needed to be reduced, and individuals had to become less selfish. Governments needed to be more far-sighted, and not constantly seeking to secure the votes in the next election, in just a couple of years' time. All this actually worked, for quite a long period anyway. The trouble is, humans are inherently defective as a species, and we seem to always throw up one more selfish and narcissistic type every now and again, and they have a remarkable ability to gain a following, and bend things to their own warped ideals. The north enjoyed two hundred and fifty years of stable, selfless government. That was good going. But then Ingersson came on the scene, and things went sour for thirty years or so..."

"Yes, I remember studying about him at school..." said Kim.

"Yes, it was a very bad time, but luckily, just a blip in the great time-scale of history. He succeeded in pitting people against each other, and souring relations with the south and Canada with a more selfish attitude, and it took quite some time after his death for international relationships to stabilise again. But since that time, we have really enjoyed a fairly blissful period."

"So did we lose much of the industrial activity that existed before the Apocalypse? And technical know-how?"

"Some, yes. Well, quite a lot in the beginning, but industries gradually revived themselves. But it was not seen as a bad thing at the time. You have to realise that the world, just before the Apocalypse, was moving forward at an unsustainable pace, and people lived the most frenetic life-styles. At least half the population of the world was able to fly wherever they wanted in the world, whenever they wanted, in these huge aircraft which emitted tons of carbon dioxide for every kilometre flown. They regarded it as their right! And they drove cars with internal combustion engines, burning refined gasoline and diesel oil like there was no tomorrow. It was madness! And no government felt that they could put a limit on any of it, because it would be bad for business. Business was the most important thing, and nothing must stop its progress. The most mundane, trivial goods were transported thousands of kilometres around the globe, with no thought for the environmental impact of that transport."

"Really? What kind of things?" asked Kim.

"Oh, stupid knick-knacks, like artificial Christmas trees and the decorations to put on them, textile goods, cars, bicycles, you name it. Things which could so easily have been produced locally!"

"How strange...!"

"Absolutely. Well, of course, all that stopped in the blink of an eye after the Apocalypse. Huge areas of vast factories in the far east and other places were destroyed or smothered in volcanic ash. Entire industries stopped dead, and the technical know-how to carry out various processes was lost for some time. Things like steel production, where you cannot let the blast furnaces cool down, ever. People where we come from had to learn to be self-sufficient extremely quickly. And to consume less. And they soon discovered that they were happier for it! They might not have had the enormous choice of goods that they'd had before, but they didn't really need it!"

"But here we are driving thousands of kilometres in this truck. Is that really so different?"

"There is a fundamental difference. All power used today is generated by ecologically sustainable means – wind, solar, geo-thermal. And there is a limit to how much we are allowed to consume. Flying is very restricted, and rationed, because it takes so much renewable power to generate the hydrogen by electrolysis. It's logical and fair to everyone..."

"I've learned so much here... Thank you Dana!"

"You're welcome! It's been like one of my seminars at the University, but with just one person."

While they were talking, the Khomas mountains had gradually become larger and clearer up ahead. The terrain was still very rugged and dry, with little hills and dips, and dry valleys winding around. They drove up little slopes, and on reaching the summit each time, the great rocky expanse revealed itself again, and the road ahead could be seen stretching away into the distance.

They had both become slightly mesmerised by the regularity of this gentle roller-coaster, and the endless ribbon of tarmac rolling out beneath them, inducing a kind of torpor. The two women were abruptly jolted out of it by a sudden flash of red colour streaking past them in the opposite direction, accompanied by a slight buffeting of the truck. As on the previous occasion, they both jumped at the unexpectedness of the meeting.

"Another despatch-rider!" said Dana. "I wonder what he's carrying..."

"Who knows?" replied Kim. "Probably nothing of interest to us..."

They reached the start of the Khomas mountains, and began climbing up winding roads again. The progress was a little slow, but they felt buoyed by the knowledge that there was only a day and-a-half or so of journey left. As the afternoon wore on, the temperature dropped a little as they gained altitude. They began to look for their overnight stopping place; there was plenty of choice, with frequent flattish areas beyond each loop in the roadway. They found a nice spot, with a great view looking back north over the lower plains. They were slightly concealed from the road by a large bush and a stunted acacia tree. They could not resist taking a little stroll through their new surroundings before settling for the evening. Dana hobbled gingerly, holding on to Kim's arm for support. There was a flat strip forming a kind of natural track in front of where they had stopped, so they walked along it for a few hundred metres. It curved round the hillside, and then to their great surprise, opened out into a large saucer-shaped area, surrounded by rocky hillocks. Incredibly, right there before them, a little stream flowed through the saucer depression, reeds swaying gently on either side. They gasped with joy at the sight, and rushed forward to dip their hands in the cool clear water. Then they were amazed to see that frogs were living in this little patch of Eden, and small birds, flitting from reed to reed. Dragonflies swooped over the water, stopping abruptly to hover for an instant, before resuming their hunts. The women looked around, then simultaneously peeled off their shoes so they could paddle in the water. After a few minutes, they sat down next to each other on a big smooth rock, and gazed in wonder at the wonderful little oasis they had stumbled across.

"Who would have thought this possible?" said Kim, "In this area which seems so arid too..."

"I know," agreed Dana, "it's just incredible; so beautiful... It must rain here now and again, and the water percolates through the rock over time. But I'm sorry to have to say that we can't stay here, unfortunately..."

"I know, I know... Maybe we could come back one day... How does your ankle feel?"

"That cool water on it was heavenly!" she replied. "I think it's helped it a bit. Maybe it will feel a lot better tomorrow. My hand has stopped throbbing now, so that's good too!"

"Thank goodness for that... I didn't let on, but I was a bit worried just after you'd done it!"

"Oh, I'm so sorry Kim... Thank you so much for looking after me..."

"You're welcome. It is my job, after all!"

"I suppose so... But I'm certainly glad that I had you there... To think that I was going to do this journey on my own originally... Thank God I found you!"

"Amen to that... I'm not sure how much further I could have got in my ancient heap of a car either. It was madness really. Imagine being stuck in some of the places we've been through..."

The women had barely paused during their whole journey except for absolutely necessary stops, so intent were they on reaching their destination. This brief respite gave them a tantalisingly brief reminder of what normal life could be like. After a while, they reluctantly tore themselves away from the scene, and returned to the truck. Dana had fretted at being out of sight of it for almost half an hour, but nothing had changed, and no-one had passed by. She set to unpacking one of their last hydrogen cells, which should let them reach their destination with a bit in reserve. Kim helped her lift it into its cubby and plug it in, then they looked at their remaining food supplies, and ate while watching the sun set.

EIGHT

GARTH

Garth was woken up by the alarm going off, together with a strange rumbling sound, and the bed shaking. He had been in a deep sleep, and felt quite disorientated. He reached for his phone on the bedside table to turn off the alarm, but it seemed to have gone. He felt for the light switch, and flipped it, but nothing happened. He sighed deeply and cursed, then swung his legs out of the bed, and stumbled over to the window to draw the curtains. The floor felt odd; it didn't seem to be level. He looked out of the window, and couldn't quite understand what he was seeing for a moment. Some of the buildings on the other side of the road seemed to have changed shape. It was very early; day was only just breaking.

After taking a couple of deep breaths and blinking a few times, Garth's focus cleared, and he understood what was in front of him. The buildings opposite had collapsed partially, and the road below him was covered in soil and debris, which was much thicker over to the left, closer to the hills.

The alarm bell was in the corridor, and continued ringing unabated. Garth suddenly felt very awake. He quickly dressed in his field clothes, and found his phone on the floor; there was still no message from Dana, and precious little signal level. He noticed now that there were small pieces of ceiling plaster strewn around the floor, and cracks in the wall. How could he not have woken up immediately the tremors started? The place must have shaken quite violently. He could not figure it out, even though Dana had always observed that he was a sound sleeper.

He went to the room door and opened it, to be deafened by the continuously ringing alarm bells. He strode along the corridor towards the stairs, and almost walked straight into another man coming out of his room.

"What the hell's going on?" asked the stranger.

"I think there's been an earthquake, and possibly a landslide" replied Garth. "Let's go and see what's happening."

"Right."

The other guy was of a similar age and height to Garth, he noticed, and sounded as though he was from the north too, judging by his accent.

They went down the stairs gingerly; they felt strange, tilted a few degrees off the horizontal, which made both men feel a bit giddy. Pieces of plaster from the ceiling lay around in here too. They reached the ground floor and turned into the reception area. There was no-one to be seen.

They opened one of the glass double doors at the front of the hotel with some difficulty, because the frame's shape had distorted, and went outside. The street's surface was invisible, totally covered in muddy soil, stones and plants, which must have slipped down from the hills to their left. The scene was like something from one of those ancient war movies, with the buildings in different states of collapse and destruction, and piles of rubble and glass leaning against their bottom floors.

"My God," cried Garth, "we're in a disaster zone!"

"It's not looking good..." said the stranger. "There must be people trapped in these buildings; we're going to have to call the emergency services, if they're not on the way already, and probably help too."

"Right," answered Garth; "let's see if the telephones work in the hotel."

They turned around. Their hotel looked almost undamaged, compared to most of the other buildings around them. They went back in, strode across to the reception desk, and lifted the phone receivers; they were all dead.

"Hello! Is there anyone here?" called Garth's companion loudly. He shouted again, louder, but there was no response.

"So what's happened to the staff?" he asked.

"Maybe they've gone to check on the guests, or their families?" answered Garth. "It's strange. My name's Garth, by the way."

"I'm Calum. I'm glad you're up and about; maybe we should stick together; what do you think?"

"Good idea. Let's just take another look out there."

The two men went outside again, heading quickly for the middle of the street, in case any debris should fall from above. There were some distant sounds of traffic, but then they also became aware of voices. Someone nearby was calling; it sounded as though these were calls for help.

They listened carefully, trying to locate the source of the calls. Whoever it was sounded weak and possibly in pain.

They went across to the other side of the street, and tried opening doors to help locate the caller. There was another small hotel opposite theirs, and they were able to wrench one of its doors open; it immediately fell off its hinges, and its large glass panel shattered into fragments as it hit the ground.

"Oops! I didn't mean to do that," Garth said, grinning.

Calum chuckled, but then they realised that the calling was coming from inside this building. They stepped cautiously inside, their shoes crunching on broken glass and plaster. The place was devastated. The calls were coming from the next level up, from what they could make out. They found the stairs, and climbed slowly and carefully, stepping over a concrete beam which had dropped from high above. The walls leaned at crazy angles, and water ran down the side of the treads.

They reached the next floor, and had to duck under fallen masonry which leaned against walls, and clamber over other sections.

"I thought these buildings were supposed to be earthquake-proof!" exclaimed Calum.

"Well, yes, but I suppose there are limits to what they can withstand..." said Garth. "And maybe the builders took some short-cuts..."

They heard the calling once again, and realised they were very close to the victim. Calum tried a door, but it was either locked from the inside or jammed. He rammed his shoulder against it, but nothing happened, except that the caller shouted out more loudly.

Garth gave the door a massive kick near its handle, and it opened partially. The two men were able to squeeze in to the room around the door.

A portly-looking man of about sixty was lying on the rubble-strewn floor, with more rubble half-covering him, as well as a large slab of concrete. The back wall of the room was missing, open to the elements.

"Oh, thank God you're here!" the man cried weakly; "I can't move..."

"All right friend, take it easy," said Calum gently, "We'll get you out of here, don't worry!"

"Don't try to move," added Garth; "we'll get all this loose stuff off you first, then see how you feel."

"OK, thank you; I'll be all right. I'm more worried about my daughter - she was in another room down the hall. Is the rest of the building OK?"

"It's not looking too good I'm afraid, but we'll take a look in a minute. Let's see if we can get the weight off you first."

Garth took a look out through the opening at the back, and ascertained that it would be safe to throw rubble into the building's back yard. The two men began gently lifting lumps of concrete, brick and plaster off the stricken man, and tossing them outside.

"What's your name, friend?" asked Calum.

"I'm Pieter, and my daughter is Lisa," he replied breathily.

"All right, hang in there, and we'll get all this crap off you. Just let us know if we're hurting you at all."

They quickly got rid of a lot of the small pieces, but the big slab was worrying them. They could barely shift it.

"We need to lever it with something," said Garth, and prop it up on some of these smaller pieces."

"Good thinking" answered Calum. "But what the hell can we use?"

"Let's try ripping one side of the door-frame out!"

"All right, but not the one to this room! It's probably helping support the walls!"

"Could well be... I'll try the one from the room opposite."

He picked up a concrete block, took it out onto the landing, and began attacking the door-frame with it, using it as a makeshift hammer. After a few whacks, it started to come away from the wall, and he was able to get hold of the bottom and lever it left and right. He succeeded in wrenching it away from the top stile, then put it on the floor to bash the protruding nails flat.

"Right, lets try this," he said.

He pushed the length of timber beneath the edge of the concrete slab, and placed the concrete block below it to act as a fulcrum. Calum got ready to push other pieces of masonry under the slab as soon as it moved. Garth pushed the end of timber downwards with all his strength, eventually standing on it to place his whole body weight on it. The wood bowed, but the slab moved upwards by a couple of centimetres or so, and Calum slipped a concrete block under it to take the weight. The old guy groaned and took gasping breaths.

"That's looking a bit better," said Garth, "but we need to raise it some more."

"Yes. But I think we need more bodies!" said Calum. "Why don't we see if anyone else has come out of hiding yet. I'll go and look out front."

"All right. I'll stay here with Pieter."

Calum went back downstairs as quickly as he dared, and out of the wrecked building. Sure enough, there was a small group of people huddled together, close by.

"Can you give us a hand please?" he called to them, "we're trying to rescue a guy who's trapped over here!"

Three men followed him quickly. One had picked up a hefty length of timber, and Calum asked him to bring it along. They climbed back up to the room where the man still lay prone, looking grey in the face.

"Pieter! Oh my God! Are you OK? We've come to get you out!" said one of the newcomers, who must have lived close by.

"Is that you Jan? I can't feel my leg, and the other one hurts like hell! But I'm still alive. But I don't know what's happened to Lisa - she was out the back here somewhere..."

"All right, we'll find her, but let's try and free you. Rick, can you go and see if Lisa needs help?" he said to to one of his companions.

That left four of them in the room with the stricken Pieter. They soon worked out a strategy to gently lift the slab of concrete, using a combination of levers and brute force. A few minutes later, they were able to slide Pieter out from underneath the masonry, and look at his wounds. He appeared to have one leg broken, while the other had a deep cut, which was bleeding heavily.

Calum had received quite extensive first aid training, and learned a few tips from Kim, his paramedic wife. He got one of the men to apply pressure close to the wound, while he rummaged through drawers to find a length of cloth of some kind. He found a tee-shirt, which he used to apply a tourniquet around Pieter's thigh.

"What we can do is tie his legs together to keep the broken one straight," he quietly told the others. "If no ambulances turn up, that is... And maybe use a length of wood as a splint."

One of the newcomers told them that he had heard that the local fire station had collapsed onto its emergency vehicles, and in any case, many of the streets were blocked by debris and masonry. They might be on their own for quite a time... Ambulances would be in great demand, the devastation being so extensive, and they were based on the far side of town anyway.

The man called Rick returned, looking serious, and gestured to Garth and Calum; they went out onto the landing, and he very quietly told them that he had found Lisa, who was also trapped. He was optimistic that she was not badly injured, but she seemed oddly quiet.

Calum crouched down next to Pieter, and told him that they had found his daughter, and that she would be fine. But they would need to go and extricate her from her room. Pieter thanked him profusely, and asked him to go to her, and not spend any more time with him.

"OK," said Calum. "But we'll come back and tell you how we're doing, and hopefully we'll get you out of here soon."

Rick led them through to a room down the landing, in which Pieter's daughter lay on the floor, covered in objects and small pieces of masonry. She appeared mostly uninjured, but did not seem very coherent. It seemed as though she might have been struck hard on the head by something falling, and might have concussion.

"Who are you? And what's happened?" she asked Calum, as he knelt down next to her.

"Hello Lisa, there's been an earthquake. Your dad is slightly hurt, but he'll be all right. We're waiting for the ambulance. We've come to help you; we'll take it very gently. My name's Calum."

"Oh, thank you. My head hurts..."

"I think you've taken a bash up there, but you're not bleeding, so don't worry! We'll get all this stuff off your legs. Hold tight!"

The men set to pulling all the detritus off the stricken woman, who winced occasionally, but bore the discomfort stoically. When she was clear, they very slowly sat her up, propping her up with pillows and cushions. She looked very pale, and complained that she felt sick. A big lump had come up at the top of her forehead.

"I think she has concussion," Calum told Garth. "Let's see if we can give her a drink; it would be a good first step. She probably hasn't had anything to eat or drink yet today..."

"Neither have we!" replied Garth. "I just thought about it..."

They found a small kitchen off the same landing. The floor was covered in pots and pans and implements, but they picked their way across to the fridge, and found partly-consumed cartons of apple and orange juice inside. Mugs hung precariously from the underside of a shelf, which dangled off the wall. They looked reasonably clean, so Calum poured a little juice into each one, and they took them through to the other room. He crouched down, and encouraged Lisa to drink some apple juice. She sipped it gratefully.

"Let's give some to Pieter too, and tell him she's OK," he said. "And then I think we should try and move them over to our hotel; I'm pretty sure that it's still structurally sound, even if its tilting very slightly - it's reinforced concrete construction." Garth concurred.

When the two victims had had a little drink, and the rescuers too, Garth gathered all the men together.

"Right, guys, we need to get a bit more organised here. I want to see how many able-bodied people are close by, and find out if there are more people who need help. Let's go back outside for a minute."

They went downstairs again, leaving Rick to keep the two victims company. There were a lot more people out in the middle of the street now, mostly just standing around, talking quietly. He walked across to them, and called over a handful of others nearby.

"Morning folks! My name's Garth, and I need your help! We've just freed two casualties in that house over there, but we need to get them out before anything more falls on them. I'd like to take them over to the hotel across there, because it looks reasonably safe. Has anyone found out if there are more people trapped? If so, we need to investigate, and form teams to free them if possible. Also, we need some sustenance! My friend here and I have been at it for nearly an hour, but haven't eaten or drunk anything since yesterday! Does anyone know if there's a shop open nearby, or can anyone bring us some coffee and a bite? Apart from that, we need some equipment, if any of you can find it; we need hard hats, shovels, crow-bars, first aid kits, and a stretcher, or something we can use as a stretcher. Then I want one or two young people who can run fast, to relay messages, as the phones are all out! And someone to just sit in the hotel and take the messages, and make sure they're relayed to us. My friend here knows some first aid, but does anyone here have some nursing experience? If we can get all these things coordinated, then we can help a lot of people! Thank you very much all of you!"

Garth seemed to have a natural leadership ability, and a charismatic personality. Calum watched him, almost open-mouthed in surprise. How had the guy thought of all these things so quickly?

The bystanders immediately seeemed to fall over each other to offer help and information. A young lad said he knew of a shop which was open, and he would go there and bring some food back. A woman offered to bring mugs of coffee, and Garth suggested they use the hotel foyer as a headquarters and meeting place. Another woman said that she knew the hotel's manager, and worked in admin; she volunteered to be the go-between in the hotel foyer. It was confirmed that the fire and rescue tenders would not be able to reach here, and that ambulances were being called from all points of town, so that they might not reach here for some hours. And the information surfaced that the disaster had been caused by a meteorite landing very close by, and initiating the earthquake.

The local people fanned out in all directions, going to find the requested equipment, and returning a little later with more helpers, all eager to play their part in the rescue efforts. Half an hour later, the hotel manager had turned up, been briefed on the plan of action, and had started organising food and drink for the volunteers. His chef had not made it in to work, so he got stuck in personally.

As if by magic, a stretcher had been located, and Calum and three others formed an interim medical team, and started the delicate operation of moving Pieter and Lisa over to the safety of the hotel, where a ground-floor room had been vacated for them.

Within another hour or so, the street and and a couple of adjacent ones had become an organised rescue scene, with Garth assuming the mantle of coordinator and technical adviser.

NINE

One of the many volunteers had eventually walked across to the ambulance base at the local hospital, and learned of the grim situation in the city. The ambulances were all out on calls all over town, and there was a back-log of requests to deal with. But he managed to persuade the receptionists to send a roving paramedic as soon as possible. It might be another hour, he was warned.

The volunteer rushed back to report this news to the go-between lady at the hotel. She in turn got one of the many young boys and girls who were acting as runners to take the news to Garth and Calum. The kids had formed their own reporting network, and knew exactly where all the main parties were at any time. Some of them had seen Calum administering his first aid, and had begun referring to him among themselves as 'Doctor Calum!' The moniker had stuck.

Around mid-morning, the paramedic arrived on an all-terrain bike, with panniers brim-full of equipment. The boys directed him across to 'Doctor Calum' in the hotel. Calum could barely contain his relief at having a proper medically-trained person to examine the casualties they had gathered in the ground-floor rooms. He took the young man, whose name was Adrian, to see the unfortunate Pieter, who had been lying untreated for about three hours by now. Adrian gave the man a pain-killing injection, and improved the support for his broken leg, but did not have the equipment to help him further.

"How long will it be before we can get him and the others to hospital?" asked Calum.

"I can't rightly say – I'm sorry," replied Adrian. "We're absolutely overwhelmed with calls... I think they have sent for support from further afield, but that will take some time to get here too. I'm afraid that we're on our own for now. But I'll stay here and help, as you seem to have set up quite a good field hospital!"

"Well, we were just lucky that this hotel is a bit more structurally sound than some of the surrounding buildings... And my new chum Garth seems to be a natural organiser."

"That's really good. Let's have a look at the other people you have brought here. We should be able to make them a bit more comfortable anyway."

Garth, meanwhile, was continuing to run the search and rescue side of the operation in the district. The locals had come up trumps with the equipment he had requested, so that they were fairly well equipped, and had no shortage of strong people to help lift and dig. One man had even brought an endoscope attachment, with a two-metre lead, which could be plugged into a cellphone. They had found that they could let this slide down through crevices in the rubble, and obtain a picture of what lay deep beneath them. It proved itself to be very useful. Every now and again, they had stopped all activity and called for silence, so they could listen out carefully for any calls for help. Miraculously, they had located and brought out a dozen casualties by late afternoon.

A little earlier, the power and telephone services had been restored. A request had been formally placed for ambulances, and they had a place in the queue. A mechanical digger had cleared a way through to the end of the road for traffic, and the first two ambulances finally arrived in late afternoon, to a rousing welcome cheer from bystanders. The paramedics set to work immediately, and gently carried the most urgent cases the short distance from the hotel to the end of the road, and very soon set off for the hospital with the first four casualties.

By nightfall, all the victims discovered so far had been taken to hospital, and Calum and Garth met up again, and could compare notes on the extraordinary day. They both felt totally drained, having barely stopped for a minute since waking up. Fortunately, the hotel manager had been a model of energy and enthusiasm, working all day long to provide food for all the volunteers that could easily be eaten on the hoof. So the guys had had food and drinks brought to them, without them even having to ask. All in all, it had been a wonderful example of humanity and cooperation in the face of adversity.

They reluctantly stopped all rescue operations soon after dark. They felt a measure of guilt at stopping, but it had quickly become clear that without light, the work was dangerous, both for the rescuers and for any casualties who might still lie undiscovered. They were both exhausted, having toiled for over twelve hours, stopping only to grab a drink and a mouthful of food on the go.

Garth and Calum returned to their rooms in the hotel, resolving to be up early to resume work. They discovered that cellphone signals had returned to a moderate level, but long-distance calls still did not work. It was very frustrating. The water pressure in the hotel was way below normal, but they were able to have a wash, and then both flaked out on their beds.

TEN

Things improved greatly the next day. A team of four men from the Fire and Rescue Service turned up around 10am. They had wheeled some specialised equipment in hand carts, since their vehicles were lying mangled under slabs of concrete at their headquarters. They were directed towards Garth, who quickly appraised them of the situation. There were still believed to be a number of people trapped in semi-collapsed buildings. In one or two cases, intermittent tapping could be heard from above when the rescuers called for silence. In other cases, it was more a case of believing that people's relatives were trapped, since they were nowhere else to be seen, and should have been in the presumed location.

A short distance from where the rescuers were operating, mechanical diggers and big trucks had been clearing away rubble and debris, and the access was almost back to normal for the area. By midday, two more casualties had been brought out of the ruins alive, albeit with horrific injuries. Adrian gave them first aid treatment, with assistance from Calum, who was quickly learning many of the essentials of field treatment for trauma. Although the work was upsetting at times, Calum had never felt so useful in his whole life, nor experienced a greater sense of satisfaction. He had quite a good career, but at the back of his mind, he occasionally wondered about how long it would take for him to retrain to be a paramedic, like Kim.

ELEVEN

DANA

The next morning, they managed to break camp fairly early. Kim felt no nausea for once, and was eager to get going, even resisting the temptation to go back to look at the stream. Dana seemed to feel a lot better now, with just a little discomfort from her ankle. She wore her shoe without any support bandaging, but gratefully let Kim take the wheel again. They got back on the road, and soon reached the highest point of the mountains, a well-eroded rounded peak, and began the descent. Below them, the land looked a bit more lush, and a few cultivated fields could be seen, very far away to the south. The road wound its way down to the plain steadily, and two hours later they were driving on an arrow-straight flat road once more.

They took a short stop for a bite of lunch, in a rather uninspiring, flat location. They had just resumed driving, when they suddenly noticed another vehicle in the far distance, coming towards them. When they had nearly reached it, the other car pulled into the centre of the road, and blue lights on its roof began to flash.

"Oh, damn!" exclaimed Kim, "We'll have to stop..."

They slowly pulled to a halt, by which time to policemen were standing in the highway, signalling to them to stop. They climbed out of the truck, and the two pairs ambled towards each other.

"Good afternoon ladies," said the stocky-looking older of the two cops. "Would you mind telling me where you have come from?"

"We've just been taking a little trip in the mountains," Dana replied. "We're entomologists from Mandela University, looking at forktail dragonfly populations up there."

"But I notice that your truck is registered in the north..."

"Yes, we moved down here earlier this year for our work," explained Dana.

"Oh, right. Can you just let us see what you're carrying in the back of your truck please? We shouldn't hold you up for long."

Dana went to the back of the truck, and unclipped the tilt cover over the cargo bay. The policeman looked in, and lifted each of the two women's holdalls, evidently appraising their weight, then slid the miscellaneous other objects around, to look in all the corners. He gestured towards the plastic water containers, and patted the two hydrogen power packs which sat at the back.

"Anticipating some extra-long drives, are you?" he asked.

"Oh, those are depleted. We still have them from when we made the journey south earlier in the year," blustered Dana, trying to retain a calm demeanour. "I keep forgetting to take them in to get my deposit back."

"You really should do that - you have quite a bit of money's-worth sitting there!"

"Yes, I must do it this week! Thanks for reminding me," she replied.

Dana noticed, with increasing nervousness, that the second cop was walking all round their truck, examining its tyres and lights, but apparently not finding any fault anywhere, though he ran a finger through the thick dust on the bonnet, and stared at it curiously for a moment. The stocky policeman then opened the truck's doors, and took a quick look inside, but nothing appeared to take his interest.

"Well, apologies for holding you up; we haven't seen much traffic this way in the last few days, so just wondered if everything was OK. We're having to stop everyone. Actually, we're on the look-out for gangs of smugglers - contraband items, you know. They're usually in small panel vans, and I'll admit that you two don't quite fit the demographic!" He chuckled.

"Oh, well we're pleased to hear that! Yes, we're fine, thank you officer. We have to make regular field trips into the mountains; we're just on our way back to the University now."

Kim thought back to the vans they saw earlier in their trip, bursting out of the tunnel mouth, and wondered, could they have been smugglers?

"That's fine then. Nice to meet you. We'll wish you ladies a great day!"

Amazingly, the cops didn't ask to see their driving licences. The women smiled sweetly at the cops, climbed back into the truck and drove gently away. Looking in the rear-view mirror, Kim could see the men standing together, looking back towards them and talking, and wondered what they might be saying.

"Oh hell, I was scared out of my wits there..." said Dana.

"Me too. So tell me, how long have you been an entomologist then, Dana?"

"Oh... About ten minutes I think..."

They burst into shrieks of laughter.

The road continued through a pleasant landscape, with slightly raised plateaus alternating with undulating areas over which its course meandered with the contours. There were small peaks here and there. A few small patches had evidently received a shower of rain in recent days, and were once again carpeted with spectacular wildflowers. It seemed strange how hit-and-miss this was, with much of the ground still retaining its arid aspect. Signposts announced a forthcoming river, the Pella. The women soon saw a large cantilever bridge up ahead, and sat forward, eager to take in this new sight. They slowed down, and peered either way along the course of the winding ribbon of blue water, flowing far below them. Cultivated fields of some kind of crop extended for some distance on the southern shore, cutting a bright green band in the surrounding parched yellow-brown countryside. But a kilometre later, the land was brown again.

***

The remainder of the day went by without further incident. The landscape rolled and looked gradually less parched. There were a few minor roads leading off east and west, snaking away into the distance. But there was also still the occasional impact crater to be seen. At the end of the day, they found a place to stop that was concealed between two small craters which lay very close to the highway. They still felt that they did not want to have a discussion with anyone about their journey; they had bluffed their way out of trouble with the police they had met, but there was no need to go looking for more trouble. Here, they would be invisible to any road-users coming from either direction until they were completely level with the gap, by which time they would be most unlikely to spot the truck.

TWELVE

The following day would be the last full day before they reached Mandela. They awoke in their private little camping space, the sun already bearing down on them from the east, and with just a few small cotton-wool balls of cloud floating here and there in an even blue sky. They had been surprised that there were no settlements yet, considering how far south they were; but the sight of these two little craters made them realise that this was still a slightly risky area in which to live. Presumably the cultivated area which they had seen alongside the river on the previous day was worked on remotely from a farm some distance further south. The two women hit the road again in their trusty truck, buoyed by the knowledge that they were almost on the last leg of their epic journey now. They still were not sure of how they would find their men once they reached Mandela, but felt confident that there would be some information available, somewhere.

They passed through very agreeable scenery, rolling gently, and dotted with healthy-looking shrubs and trees. Once again, there were occasional patches of spectacular wildflowers, and it was hard to believe that they had not been planted deliberately by somebody, long ago. The day was unremarkable in its normality, until the early afternoon.

They were cruising along at speed, coming around a slight curve in the road. When it straightened out, they were taken aback to see the hazy outline of a city in the distance ahead of them. It was puzzling; there should not be any settlement for another 600 kilometres, when Mandela would come into view below mountains. Kim consulted her tablet, examining the maps closely as Dana drove on. Eventually, she found the explanation for this mirage; this was the abandoned city of Kenhart.

Sixty years earlier, there had been a respite from the annual bombardment of meteorites landing on the planet from outer space. For five years, there were no impacts. There was a great rejoicing, and many people celebrated by taking long tours into the central belt during the usual meteorite season, despite scientists' warnings that this was undoubtedly a temporary lull. There was such a conviction among many that the planet was a completely safe place once more, that speculative builders began planning, and then constructing, a new city far to the north of Mandela. There was a shortage of housing at the time, and a thirst for new sites for industry, and so Kenhart had come to be built in a very short space of time. People moved there, sensing new opportunities and a clean new place to live. And then, the meteorites had struck again. The scientists had been right; the path of the meteorite belt had merely swung to a slightly different alignment for a few years, in a natural cycle which recurred every two centuries, but it had now returned to its former trajectory. It was a disaster, although there had been mercifully few casualties when the first meteorites struck. But there had been an immediate mass exodus from the new city, and the place had been abandoned forever.

Kim and Dana found it impossible not to slow down and gaze at the eery sight of this modern ghost-town. Numerous office and apartment blocks looked quite intact, but others had partially collapsed as a result of the tremors caused by a meteorite impacting close-by. A couple of buildings had received a direct hit, and lay in a big heap of rubble. Others had lost their windows, which had been shaken out by the tremors. They could see neatly laid-out roads running between buildings, but beginning to be taken over by plants, grasses and small trees. Tall lamp-posts leaned over at crazy angles.

It was a very sad sight, and they felt no desire to go and take a closer look.

The day was fairly uneventful after this. They pushed on. They began to see one or two other vehicles gradually, but no-one seemed to take the slightest notice of them, so they felt fairly relaxed. There were more and more roads leading off each side, and signposts giving directions to small settlements. Rows of electricity pylons had been erected parallel to the highway, carrying the power to these places from unseen solar farms. They were back in civilisation.

That evening, they turned off the main road, and found a secluded and concealed place among trees to spend their last night before they reached the big city.

THIRTEEN

The women slept less well that night, fretting about what the next day would bring, and how they would go about their search. They both spent a long time mulling over the possibilities, and their various fears, before dropping off to a fitful, disturbed sleep.

They revived themselves in the morning with strong coffee and tea. Kim had suddenly taken a strong dislike to coffee, which she had always loved. Luckily though, she no longer felt nauseous in the mornings.

The last stretch leading to Mandela looked very much like familiar territory for them: more and more tracts of abundantly fertile farmland, wineries too, interspersed with huge solar farms, and row upon row of enormous wind turbines perched on the higher ground. They felt a measure of excitement and relief at returning to civilisation, after so many long days of traversing endless dusty wilderness, as well as a feeling of elation at having succeeded in this madcap journey, and conquered this gigantic continent. On the down-side, the traffic was increasing steadily on the two-lane highway, and they realised that they would be arriving in the city just at the start of the rush hour, which would not help their frayed nerves.

On reaching Mandela, they noticed some slight damage to some of the buildings, presumably from an earthquake. This gave them a valuable insight into the possible events of the past few weeks in this region. Could this be the underlying reason for communications and travel between the north and the south having stopped for so long? They soon ground to a halt in the city traffic, which gave them the chance to admire the attractive architecture, and watch people walking along pavements, for the first time in eight days. It was surprising how pleasant an activity this could be after the isolation of the desert belt. Even so, what they wanted above all was to stop driving, and begin the search for their loved ones. Mandela was a big city; maybe not as large as Laxberg, but still a huge conurbation, with a high-rise central business district. They needed to find somewhere to stay before becoming ensnarled in city-centre traffic. They turned off the main artery leading into the centre, and found a quiet district of small hotels and guest houses. They picked at random a modest but nicely maintained guest house, which turned out to be run by a very pleasant middle-aged couple originally from the north, Maxine and Trevor, who made no observations about their dusty, slightly dishevelled appearance. Trevor showed them to their twin room, and, having noticed their very obvious fatigue, prepared a tray of tea and cakes for them while they cleaned up a bit.

After an initial hesitancy, they revealed to their hosts over the welcome hot drink the reason for their epic journey; the hosts' faces showed a mixture of horror and admiration at what the two women had faced to arrive here. Trevor explained that there had been two meteorite strikes beyond the end of the normal season, and much further south than usual. The second of these had struck the city of Swellendam, 250 kilometres east of Mandela, and triggered an earthquake and a landslide. There had been significant loss of life and destruction. Could this be the reason for the continuing closure of the highways, and the loss of communications, they wondered? The prolonged solar flare activity must also have played a part in the comms black-out, they realised. The rumours of civil unrest had just been a red herring. The two young women blanched on learning this news, but Maxine and Trevor did their utmost to reassure them that the problem was most likely just a loss of contact, and that it was

very unlikely that their husbands were casualties. Maxine, clucking over them like a favourite aunt, gave them the directions to Mandela's main hospital and the central Police Headquarters, and offered to help in any way that she could to find Garth and Calum. Dana and Kim immediately felt that they had two new allies in their quest. It felt so good to have this support.

Threading their way through the huge city, they located the main hospital; Being a medic, Kim understood the workings of a hospital, and made straight for the reception desk, bypassing protocols, and somehow making the receptionist believe that she worked in this facility. All the region's medical centres were linked in a common computer system; the receptionist cut no corners in examining every possible way of tracking the two men, but found no record at all of Garth or Calum. That was good news, in a way. They moved on to the central police station, but, ominously, found a very long queue of people waiting outside it. Feeling dead-beat, they decided reluctantly to return in the morning. They ate in a pizza place; it seemed as though it should be an amazing treat after all the days on the road with camp-food, but they just could not summon the enthusiasm to really enjoy their meal; they just chewed mechanically because they needed to, although the accompanying fresh green leaves felt surprisingly welcome. They returned to the guest-house, feeling rather down-cast, but savoured the luxury of a long shower, and collapsed into amazingly soft and comfortable beds. For the first time in eight nights, they were able to stretch their legs out full-length.

FOURTEEN

The next morning, they awoke fairly early, because they had settled into this rhythm by now. Trevor made them a hearty breakfast, while Maxine asked them how they had fared the previous evening. Feeling slightly more human, and dressed more respectably, Dana and Kim then made their way back to the police station. They joined a long queue at the inquiries desk, behind a number of other people, all anxiously awaiting their turn in silence.

When they eventually reached the front of the queue, and asked for news of Calum Johnson and Garth Mirey, there was a puzzling, instant reaction from the sergeant at the desk; he went wide-eyed for the shortest moment, and then the tiniest flash of a smile crossed his face for a millisecond. They could almost have missed it, but it was definitely there. He turned around, and called through a doorway to a constable sitting at a desk in the office behind, in which a dozen or so policemen and women were evidently fielding endless phone calls. He turned back, and said "I think we may have some news for you. My colleague will look after you."

"Can you please just tell us if they are alive and well?" pleaded Dana.

"I'm afraid that I don't have the latest information to hand; I am sorry. But I happen to know that they survived the meteorite strike and the landslide. But things are unfolding rapidly. If you go with my colleague, he will tell you all we know."

The second officer asked them to follow him down a long corridor, and they were shown into a small interview room. The man had a pleasant manner, and was very polite towards them, but they still felt great anxiety.

"Could you just wait here a moment please. I'll be right back. I think we will have some intel for you."

The women's stomachs lurched, but the man had been smiling and friendly; and the desk officer had talked of good news, hadn't he? Or did he just say 'news'?...

An Inspector came along with the junior desk officer after a couple of minutes. He was immaculately dressed, and spoke with a very strong southern accent. He asked why they were inquiring about Dr Johnson and Mr Mirey, and asked them to produce identity documents.

"Mr Calum Johnson" said Kim; he's not a doctor."

"We're talking about Calum Bjorn Johnson? Is that right?" said the Inspector. "From Kristiansand, Laxberg Province?"

"That's right; my husband," replied Kim.

"Right. Doctor Calum Johnson," repeated the Inspector. "That's what we have him down here as."

"No, my husband is a civil engineer, working for Nor-Vatten!" Kim retorted. "Look, please can you just tell us if he and Garth Mirey are well?"

"We believe that they were fine three days ago, as long as we are talking about the same people. But there's been a lot happening... Now, do you have a photograph of him on you?"

"Yes, I have lots, here in my phone" she said, reaching into her bag. She opened the photo gallery in the device, found some recent images of Calum, and handed the phone over to the Inspector. He looked at the screen, and angled the device for his junior to see.

"That's Doctor Johnson OK," confirmed the policeman, comparing the picture with one on a document he was holding. "At least, that's who we believe him to be. And can you show us a photo of Garth Mirey?" he asked, turning to Dana.

She already had her phone in her hand, and had located a good, recent shot of Garth. The policeman looked at it, compared it to a photo on a tablet, and nodded to his superior.

"I don't understand the 'doctor' part," said Kim, "but please, just tell us if Garth and Calum are alive and well, and what happened to them?"

The Inspector looked at them both, and leaned forward, resting his forearms on the table between them.

"Your husbands were staying in a hotel in Swellendam, about 250 kilometres east from here. There was a small meteorite strike very close by, which resulted in the collapse of several buildings. A landslide followed, set off by the ensuing tremor. We know that Dr Johnson and Mr Mirey survived the incident with maybe just a few scrapes, and have been helping with rescue efforts in the city. Unfortunately, communications are rather patchy, because phone masts were brought down by the incident, and the city is in total chaos still. So I'm afraid we cannot tell you their current whereabouts. It's not a very safe place to travel to either, I must warn you."

"So what are we supposed to do now?" asked Kim. "Are you getting updates about visitors like them?"

"The news we receive is rather sporadic I fear," said the Inspector. "And we are being inundated with requests from the public for information, as you could see back there. But if we have your contact details, we can let you know if we hear anything. That's about as much as we can do. But before you leave, can you please tell me how and when you got here? There are no flights from Laxberg currently."

"We drove down here," said Dana, after a moment's hesitation.

"You *drove*?" cried the Inspector, a shocked expression etched on his face. "But, are you crazy? That's 11,000 kilometres!"

"12,770, actually," stated Kim. "The thing is, nobody would give us any information, so we thought we'd come and ask you!"

"But we've just had the meteorite season, wasn't this a rather irresponsible venture?" asked the junior policeman, "not to mention – against the law...!"

"I think we both know that the season has passed, but for some reason the all-clear has not been given. We could have waited weeks for information; the authorities in Laxberg move like setting lava..."

"Very well," said the Inspector, after considering the matter quietly for a moment. "Let's forget about that. I believe that a lot of people in Swellendam owe your husbands a lot of thanks, so I'm going to help you as much as I can."

He went on to explain that Garth and Calum had shown great initiative in helping to rescue people trapped in collapsed buildings in Swellendam. The fire station in the city had been destroyed by the landslide, and a number of streets had been blocked by debris, so that rescue efforts had had to be undertaken by private citizens. It seemed that the two men had been instrumental in coordinating the first response to the disaster, and were held in very high regard there.

The two women looked at each other briefly, surprise and pride on their faces.

"So why was the all-clear for the H2 highway not given earlier?" asked Dana, finally.

"That was because there was another meteorite strike, before the one which hit Swellendam, about two weeks ago. It was a bit further north, but still south of the expected area, and obviously, also beyond the normal end of the 'season.' Added to that, we still had problems with the exceptional solar flare activity, so news was rather slow at being forwarded north. I shouldn't really say this, but the government down here can be a bit slow with passing on information, or at least the details. But I imagine that you may well have crossed paths with the news while you were travelling southwards! I have to say that it's not that wise really to take things into your own hands as you have done..."

Dana kept quiet at this point, feeling some embarrassment. Yes, maybe she had been a bit impetuous, but no harm had come from it, fortunately. And in any case, she might still have been sitting at home at this point, still waiting for news of Garth, since telecoms were not yet fully functioning. At least she now knew that he was alive and well...

Dana and Kim left the police station, after filling in forms with their contact details, as well as those of the guest-house, and pondered their next move. They were desperate to move on to Swellendam, despite the policemen's entreaties to stay in Mandela. They had kept trying to make contact with Garth and Calum, but could not get any response from their messages. They decided to go back to the guest-house, and talk to Maxine and Trevor.

By the time they had returned to their temporary base, it was nearly lunch-time. Trevor invited the women to come and watch the television news with him in their lounge, while Maxine made some sandwiches for them all.

The second feature on the news was all about the post-quake rescue efforts ongoing in Swellendam. There was drone footage of collapsed and badly damaged buildings, and the hillside with a chunk missing from the landslide. The piece then cut to a reporter on the ground, standing in front of a scene of devastation, with people in the background sifting through wreckage and rubble, describing the rescue operations. He talked about how the vital rescue services had initially been prevented from reaching some of the areas affected, because of the landslide and the destruction of the fire station, and how local volunteers had stepped in to the chaos, and organised their own rescue operation. In particular, he said, local officials had heaped high praise on two young visiting workers, one of whom was originally from Dontsane, and who had set up a remarkable organisation, and mobilised and motivated local people with enormous success, rescuing twenty people so far. The camera shot cut to a recorded interview of the two heroes, whom the journalist introduced as Garth Mirey and Dr Calum Johnson.

"KIM! Oh my God, IT'S THEM! Look! It's Calum and Garth! I don't believe it!" yelled Dana.

"No way!" said Kim simply, her gaze transfixed by the sight of Calum, calmly talking on the television.

"Maxine!" called Trevor, "come and see this! It's the two lads!"

Maxine rushed through from the kitchen, wiping her hands on her apron, and the four of them watched in amazement as Garth and Calum answered questions about their involvement in the rescue operations, the difficulties they still faced, and the condition of some of the victims. When the interviewer asked them about where they came from, and why they were working in the region, Calum mentioned that they had wives and family back home whom they had been unable to contact in over eight weeks, and made a plea for help in reassuring their loved ones that they were safe. The journalist promised to try to make it happen. The piece ended.

"Unbelievable..." said Kim. "Oh, thank God... I thought I might never see him again..."

Dana crouched down next to her, and the two wrapped their arms around one another, tears rolling down their cheeks.

***

As they ate their lunch with Maxine and Trevor, Dana and Kim were already thinking about the next stage of their journey. They *had* to go to Swellendam, even if the police Inspector had advised against it. They would not be a burden on local services: for the previous eight days, they had shown that they could be self-sufficient, eating by the side of the road, and sleeping in the truck. Having come this far, they had to go these last 250 kilometres to find their men. They could even be useful, if there was still a need by the time they arrived. After all, Kim was a paramedic, and had a good amount of her equipment aboard the truck. Dana seemed to fully fit again now, and could surely help in some way.

Maxine and Trevor listened to the two young women discussing their plan of action without raising any doubts or concerns. They had seen how determined and capable these two were, and realised that it would be pointless trying to stop them. If anything, they wanted to help the two couples to be reunited; the 'girls' had brought a bit of excitement into their lives, and they felt an attachment to them.

"If you come back through Mandela on your way home, please come and stay with us! Said Maxine. "We'd love to meet your husbands. You can even come and stay here for free for a night or two if you like!"

"Good idea!" added Trevor. "But whatever happens, stay in touch. We'd love to hear how you get on."

With that, they had gone to pack their bags. Kim decided to try her phone again. To her surprise, it started ringing normally. After a slight delay, suddenly, there was Calum, speaking from the other end, his face filling the screen.

"Hello? Is that you Kim?"

"YES! Are you OK? Oh Calum, goodness, it's been so long! I've been so worried about you!"

"I'm fine, thanks, but it's a bit chaotic down here. There's been an earthquake... Are you all right?"

"I'm fine, apart from having been worried sick! I know about the earthquake, we saw you on television just a little while ago!"

"You did? Who's 'we'? I can't believe they would show us on TV back home!"

"No, no, we're in Mandela!"

"In Mandela? Who is? How on earth did you get there? I thought all travel was suspended still..."

"We drove down! Listen, do you have a friend there called Garth? Because I'm with his wife, Dana!"

"What? Really? How on earth did you meet her? But you couldn't have driven down here, it would take days!"

"We did! We met up on the road, and drove down together in her truck. It took eight days!"

"NO! Kim, you're mad! But wasn't it dangerous? I thought there were still meteorites flying around..."

"We didn't see any. And the roads were nice and quiet! Listen, we're fine, absolutely fine, but we desperately want to see you both. Look, I'm just going to get Dana. Is Garth there?"

"Well, he's somewhere around here, but there's a lot going on; we're still digging people out of the wreckage here..."

"Look, just try and find him, and I'll get Dana to ring him. It seems as though the phones are working again at last. We're going to drive over from Mandela. We should be there in a bit over three hours if we set off soon."

"Oh, gosh, Kim, is that a good idea? It's total destruction down here..."

"You're not going to stop us! We can help, remember. I'm a medic, and Dana is quite practical, and we can sleep in the truck if need be; we've been doing that for the last eight days..."

"Yes, well that makes sense I suppose. I'm just a bit taken aback that you're so close by! But, yes, come on over, the more the merrier! I'll go and find Garth, and tell him to expect a call. God, I love you, Kim! I can't wait to see you!"

"I love you too! Now, just tell me how to find you two guys, and we'll get on our way soon!"

Calum gave Kim the directions for the hotel, and she went to find Dana, who was trying to settle up their bill with Maxine. Dana could barely contain her excitement when she learned that Kim had got through to Calum, and that Garth would be expecting a call. She rushed back upstairs to phone from their room, while Kim asked Maxine for directions to a food store. They would need to buy a few provisions before hitting the main roads, as there was a slight risk of shortages in Swellendam.

They set off soon after. Maxine and Trevor waved them off, with Maxine making them promise to come back to visit. They bought their essential provisions, found the city's ring road, and then the highway to Swellendam.

The women were both experiencing a massive rush of elation and excitement, tempered by a desire to be extra-cautious in this final leg before they were reunited with their loved ones. It would not do to have some kind of mishap at this eleventh hour...

"I almost can't believe that this is happening, Dana... The last eight days have felt more like a month!"

"I know... We've seen some incredible things, haven't we?"

"One or two! So, was Garth OK about us doing this crazy trip, or was he mad at you?"

"I think he was a bit surprised, to say the least! And maybe worried about his precious truck. But I think I know a way to win him round."

"I wonder what that might be?" replied Kim, with a little giggle.

"You haven't told Calum about the baby yet, have you?" asked Dana.

"No, I thought I'd keep that for face-to-face. One shock at a time is enough!"

Dana chuckled.

The road to Swellendam took them through lush, rolling farmland of huge fields, with distant ranges of big hills. It was very lovely, but their minds were a jumble of confused thoughts about the past few days, and the coming ones. They were a bit apprehensive about the sights that might greet them in the stricken city, but also anxious to help out as much as they could. It would be another new experience, that was for sure.

They drove steadily without stopping, and after two and a half hours, Swellendam came into view in the distance. Dana was driving, while Kim picked up her tablet to check on their final destination. From a distance, the city looked quite normal; but as they got close, they began to notice little signs of damage. The road was cracked right across its width here and there, although not enough to cause a problem, and older houses in the outer suburbs had windows and roof tiles missing, and one even had its whole roof shaken out of alignment with the walls below. When they reached the city proper, they could see damage on an altogether bigger scale everywhere. It was an awful sight. Then they saw the first collapsed buildings. These were mostly older structures, which had not been built to the standards demanded now. The reality of the sight was so much more shocking than pictures seen on television, and made them think with distress about the possible fate of the occupants. They drove the remainder of the way in silence, interspersed only with muted groans when another scene of destruction struck them.

They reached a point quite close to the street where Garth and Calum's hotel-cum-field-hospital stood, but the roads were blocked by temporary barricades. Workmen stood guard to allow through emergency vehicles only. They parked in an adjacent street, which looked strangely unaffected by the disaster, and walked the rest of the way, Kim bringing her medical kit. When they reached the street, it was a hive of activity. There were emergency vehicles parked here and there, and a mechanical digger and large trucks, loading up rubble. A number of workmen were hard at it, clearing smaller debris with shovels, and one or two groups of boys and girls aged between about ten and fourteen stood to one side, surveying the scene.

The workmen were too busy to take any notice of Kim and Dana, so Kim went up to the nearest group of youngsters, and asked where the Nelson Hotel was.

"I'm looking for a man called Calum, who's helping here..."

The kids' faces lit up with broad smiles.

"You want Doctor Calum? We'll take you to him. Come with us lady!"

A boy and a girl led the way at speed, Kim and Dana trailing in their wake, and called out eagerly to the other kids "...visitors for Doctor Calum...!"

Dana turned to Kim and said - "Well, someone's got a fan-club here..."

Kim laughed. "Do you think it's these kids who invented this whole 'Doctor' thing?"

"I'm getting that idea..."

The small party walked into the hotel, and the boy and girl led Kim and Dana up to the reception desk, where the go-between lady was still sitting, relaying messages and organising things.

"Mrs Slater - visitors for Doctor Calum!" announced the boy. "These two ladies!"

"Oh, thank you very much, Jason. While you're here Jason, can you just take this message to Mr Garth?"

"Yes, Mrs Slater, of course!"

"Just a minute," piped up Dana, "do you mean Garth Mirey? Only I'm his wife, and I've just arrived here. If you mean him, can you take me to him as well?"

"Oh, goodness! Are you Garth Mirey's wife? How lovely to meet you! Oh, he's going to be thrilled! Jason, take the lady and this message to Mr Garth right away."

"I'll meet you back here in a while," Dana called back to Kim as she followed the boy.

"It seems our husbands are quite the celebrities around here..." said Kim to Mrs Slater.

She laughed, then said "Oh, yes. They've been wonderful! Calum is just down the corridor here, with a patient. Follow me..."

Kim followed the kindly old lady along the ground-floor corridor. Just as they were nearing a door, it opened, and Calum emerged with a paramedic. He looked up, saw Kim, and stopped dead in his tracks.

"Doctor Johnson, I presume?" said Kim.

"KIM! You're here! I can't believe it...!"

They fell into each other's arms, hugged one another hard, and kissed. Kim's cheeks were running with tears, and she was unsure whether to laugh or cry. Mrs Slater and the paramedic crept away quietly, broad smiles on their faces, but looked back surreptitiously to take in the happy reunion.

"Oh Calum... I was so worried! I just couldn't work out what might have happened... It's so good to be here with you..."

"It's OK sweetheart. But, oh, it's been such a weird time, and I'm so tired..."

"I can imagine. Well I'm here, and I can help. But also, I have some news for you!"

Back at the reception desk, Mrs Slater and the paramedic heard a yell and a whoop, and looked at each other questioningly. They each chuckled, then shrugged, and decided not to intrude into the couple's moment of privacy.

After asking Kim about a hundred questions, Calum, wearing a broad grin on his face, gave her a brief run-down of the events of the last few days, and explained how they had used the hotel as a field hospital and triage centre initially. Now, they were just using it to house casualties temporarily, before ambulances took them away to the hospital. But he had also treated and dressed countless minor injuries, using first aid equipment supplied by local people and the hotel. Things were calming down considerably now, and they were not sure whether any more victims of the quake still remained to be found. Garth had taken the lead at the beginning of the search and rescue operation, and many locals had just assumed that this was his area of expertise, and followed his direction willingly.

Calum took Kim into an adjacent room, to meet Adrian, the other paramedic, who was talking to a casualty, and re-dressing his wound.

"It's great to meet you Kim," he said. "You've arrived at the tail-end of this thing, or at least I hope so! But we may still find one or two more people. Anyway, it's good to have some reinforcement!"

"I'm glad to be here," replied Kim. "You have no idea how glad I am!"

Things gradually quietened down outside, as daylight began to fade. An ambulance rolled up outside the hotel, and the two patients were transferred to it, leaving Adrian, Calum, and Kim with nothing to do for the time being. They sat on the sofas in the reception area, and related their recent adventures to each other.

Searching continued right into that night, because one of the rescuers thought he had heard a tapping noise, coming from about the only wrecked building not to have been investigated. By this time, portable floodlights had been brought in to enable round-the-clock working. Time was critical now.

Following her own joyful and emotional reunion with Garth, Dana had immediately got stuck into helping with the search efforts. Kim and Calum had come along to the rescue site, waiting to see if anyone was brought out of the ruins, so that they could give medical aid without delay. Adrian had gone home, having already worked over twelve hours that day.

It was just after one o'clock in the morning when a young boy of about six years of age was brought out of the rubble. He had been trapped, but remarkably was relatively uninjured, aside from extensive bruising, and dehydration. But he pleaded with the rescuers to find his grandmother, who was still trapped somewhere close to where he had been. She had been able to call out encouragement to the boy from time to time, and had kept up occasional bouts of tapping to try and summon help. Worryingly, he had not heard anything of her in the last hour or so.

An hour later, the grandmother was located, and was brought out soon after. She had terrible crush injuries, and a broken arm. Kim and Calum were there, and were able to give first aid immediately. The old lady, whose name was Miriam, was gently carried back to the hotel, where Kim quickly inserted a cannula into the back of her hand, and set up a drip to rehydrate her. She woke up after a few minutes, and Kim was able to tell her that her grandson was alive and well, and in an adjoining room, awaiting transport to the hospital.

They had given Miriam a morphine injection, to make her feel a little more comfortable, and once it had taken effect, they carried her as gently as possible to the ambulance outside. Kim sat with her while the other paramedics went to fetch the second casualty. Miriam had stayed conscious throughout, although she closed her eyes some of the time.

In the ambulance, she looked up at Kim, and said: "You had a very long journey across the desert to find your soulmate..."

"Yes, did he tell you that?"

"No, I saw it..."

Kim frowned, not understanding.

"You are going to have a baby soon..."

"Yes! I didn't think it showed at all yet!"

"Oh no, not at all..."

"So was that a guess?" asked Kim.

"No... I... I could tell." Miriam took a few deep breaths, clearly still in great pain.

"You will see a heart in the eastern sky, and then the baby will come. It will be a boy. He will become a good man, a great leader. He will look very much like your father did."

"My father passed away two years ago..."

"Yes, in April. He was a good man. He is very proud of you."

"I don't understand... Do you know my family?"

"No..."

"Then how do you know about my father? It doesn't make sense..."

"Everything is written in the stars... As your son will know."

Kim was totally confused. Was this woman suffering from drug-induced delirium, or plain psychotic? How had she guessed that Kim was pregnant? She was on the point of asking her another question when the two paramedics arrived, carrying the young boy on a stretcher, and she had to quickly get out of their way. When they had secured the new arrival, Kim just had time to mount the back step of the ambulance, and call in to the old lady:

"Good bye Miriam; I hope that you get well quickly. Good luck!"

"Thank you my dear. God bless you for your care. Take care of yourself, and that little one..."

Kim watched the ambulance drive away, and stared after it until it had turned the corner.

Rescue operations stopped for the night. The four young people were all exhausted, but felt a surge of elation following the last two rescues, as well as great happiness from being reunited with each other. There were things that needed to be discussed and arranged, but they could wait until the next day.

FIFTEEN

The Mayor of Swellendam came to meet the rescuers the next morning, and thank them in person for their magnificent efforts. He even invited them to visit him at his office the following day.

Kim had asked Calum to come with her to the hospital. She wanted to find out how Miriam and her grandson were doing, and she wanted the old lady to see the two of them together. She had told Calum about the strange things that Miriam had said; he had been highly sceptical, attributing her words to a fever, or the morphine, or both, but had not felt that he could leave Kim to go and make the visit on her own. Kim desperately wanted to talk to Miriam again, and was hoping that maybe she would glean a little more understanding of the old lady's extraordinary insight. They had walked the two miles to the hospital, and asked for directions to the ward where Miriam was being treated. They went up a lift, and along a corridor, and located the nurses' station at the head of the ward. They asked to see Miriam, who had been brought in the previous night.

The Nursing Sister looked at them for a moment, then said quietly "I am so sorry, but I have to tell you that Miriam passed away about an hour ago. I'm afraid that she had some severe internal injuries..."

SIXTEEN

The rescue operation had finished, and the four young people were beginning to recover from the extreme fatigue they were feeling, following all their strenuous efforts, as well as the arduous travelling in Dana and Kim's case. Garth and Calum both yearned to get away from the constant scenes of destruction which had been surrounding them for more than a week. The four of them had managed to enjoy a meal or two in restaurants, in a city centre area which seemed unaffected by the earthquake, and had found that they really enjoyed each other's company. Both Calum and Garth's work projects were being shelved for the time being, pending geological reports to assess the stability of the area of their proposed works. Before heading back north, Garth wanted to take Dana to visit his parents in Dontsane, which was 800 kilometres east of Swellendam, but did not feel happy to abandon Calum and Kim just yet. He knew the region around Swellendam quite well, having grown up not that far away, and so he suggested to the others one evening that they should take a little ride out north the next day, into a former wildlife reservation area. He promised them that it would be green and hilly and very pleasant, and observed that it would do them all good to spend a day in nature again. The others all agreed that it sounded like a lovely idea to get out of town, take a gentle tour, guided by someone with local knowledge, and try to forget about the impending return to work for another day.

After a leisurely breakfast the next morning, they set off eastwards initially, and after passing the ubiquitous solar farms, drove through productive looking farmland, with a range of mountains away to their left. After a few miles, they turned left onto a smaller road, which took them gradually closer to the foot of the mountains. All looked normal, aside from the occasional crack across the roadway, testament to the recent meteorite-induced earthquake. Five miles on, Garth turned left at a T-junction, onto another small road, which began climbing up into the high ground. Dana was sitting next to him in the front passenger seat, while Calum and Kim sat in the back, holding hands, enjoying the ride. Kim remarked that it was strange to be sitting in the back, but that it was nice to let someone else take total charge. As soon as they had turned off the main road, the scenery immediately became stunningly beautiful; the narrow road wound in a series of tight hairpin bends, climbing all the way, following the snaking line of a small river, way below them to the left. There were great expanses of bare rock, but plants and small shrubs clung to the hillsides wherever they could anchor themselves, and exotic-looking flowering shrubs bloomed profusely at the roadsides. From time to time, they caught sight of fast-flowing water and cascades way below them, but there was nowhere to stop safely, and no safe path down to the torrent. A group of small rocky pinnacles rose up close to the road on the right. They all exclaimed at how beautiful this road was, and thanked Garth for suggesting the idea of this little trip.

After about five miles of climbing, the road levelled out, and then began winding down towards another wide plain, but at a higher level than the previous one. They came to a T-junction at a slightly wider road, and turned right, heading east again, travelling through a very broad U-valley, with a great vertical escarpment off to the left. This area was more rugged than earlier on, and not suitable for any kind of farming. The road gradually curved round towards the north, heading for another range of small mountains. It was gloriously wild country all around. But sinister cracks could still be seen here and there in the tarmac and across the ground.

"Not too much further," said Garth, and then we can take a walk in a nice part."

"That sounds good," replied Kim. "It's really gorgeous around here."

Ten miles on, the road forked, and they turned left, now heading more or less due north. The rugged scenery continued, the road diving into shallow hollows and climbing out again, slowly curving round to a westerly direction now, with a line of hills off to the right. They began to drive alongside a little river, which evidently flowed with a far greater volume at times, judging by the broad bed of large stones and rocks that it trickled through. The water-course flowed closer and closer to the foot of a fairly steep slope, at the base of the line of hills. The hillside was similar to the part they had ascended earlier, with bare rock in places, but healthy-looking little shrubs and flowering plants clinging to the side. It clearly rained regularly here. They came to a place where a steep and narrow cleft was carved into the mountainside, with a small stream flowing down it. Garth stopped the truck on a flat grassy area next to the road.

"Right, folks, here we are. If I remember rightly, this is a really nice path!"

They got out of the truck eagerly, donning small back-packs, in which they had stowed some food and drink for a picnic. It was a lovely warm day, with just a few small scattered clouds in an otherwise perfectly blue sky. Garth, hand-in-hand with Dana, led the way towards the track, Kim and Calum following close behind. The path immediately began to climb quite steeply, parallel to the stream, which cascaded over and around large smooth rocks. Insects of all kinds buzzed around them, sometimes chased by large dragonflies. Small birds criss-crossed the stream, perching on rocks close to the water's edge, diving in now and again, while large raptors could be seen high overhead, soaring in great spirals.

"This is so lovely!" Kim said to Calum. "It's so nice to be in nature again."

"Yes, I needed this, I must say. It's been a bit grim over the last few days..."

They continued upwards at a gentle pace, which nevertheless had their hearts beating much harder than normal. All was lovely and normal around them, excepting for the occasional crack in the ground, which bothered Garth a little. He had not expected to see this evidence of the 'quake so far east of the strike point. After half an hour, they stopped briefly for a drink, sitting on rocks quite close to the stream, and taking in the view back down to where they had set off.

Ten minutes further up the track, they were surprised to see large rocks which had evidently tumbled from higher up very recently. Some had landed right in the stream, forcing it to divert its course around the new obstruction. They pressed on, but Garth was increasingly gaining the impression that something big had occurred above where they were walking. It was unexpected, but even so, he didn't think it should affect them too much. If they found that the path was blocked at some point, they could simply stop and go back down; they would still have enjoyed a nice walk.

The ground levelled out slightly, and they were able to see a bit further ahead. There was a large flat area just a short distance in front of them, and then the hillside climbed to a second crest some way beyond that. But then they noticed that there was a big new ugly scar in the distant crest, where there had clearly been a landslide. When they reached slightly further on, they could see the spoil from this avalanche lying in a huge untidy pile at the far side of the flat area. It was a great jumble of huge chunks of rock, mixed with soil and uprooted shrubs, devastating the previously perfect scene.

"Oh, what a shame," said Dana. "I don't think we'll be able to go very much further. The path has been obliterated..."

"It might not be too safe around here anyway," replied Garth. "I'm a bit worried about further landslips. The ground has become a bit unstable following the 'quake..."

They carried on into the wide flat clearing, looking upwards all around them cautiously for any tell-tale signs of possible slipping. Not that they would really be able to spot anything; the ground would just suddenly start moving without warning, and they would have to run.

"I think I can hear something," said Kim suddenly. "Or someone."

They strained their ears, but heard nothing. Then Calum heard it too. It sounded as though someone was calling, up ahead near where the landslide material was lying. They moved forward another hundred metres or so, and stopped to listen again. Nothing. Looking ahead, they were surprised to see the remains of a big fence crossing the landscape, surrounding much of this flat area. It looked fairly new, but a long section of it had been swept some distance by the tumbling debris of the earthfall.

"What on earth is a fence doing up here?" asked Garth. "This is a nature reserve... It doesn't make sense."

They walked a little further, and then all of them simultaneously heard the voice. It was somebody calling weakly for help, somewhere up ahead of them. They rushed forwards towards the source of the sound, but could not see anyone. They began calling to whoever might be there, and then heard a reply.

"Over to the left there I think," said Dana, "near that big rock."

The four of them headed for the place where the voice seemed to have come from, unable to see anyone amongst the rocks and debris. Then Kim spotted a man, lying on the ground, half-covered in soil and rocks. His clothes were filthy from the soil he had been rolled through, making him difficult to spot.

"Over there!" she called to the others. "There's a guy half-buried."

They rushed over to the prone figure. It was a man in his mid-forties, looking in a bad state. His face was grey, and his features drawn.

"Oh hell, here we go again!" exclaimed Garth. "I thought we'd finished with digging people out."

They all set to uncovering the man, who had a number of fairly large pieces of rock lying across his legs.

"Just stop a minute," said Kim, "let's give him some water before we do any more."

"Good idea," agreed Dana.

They held his head up a little, and put a water bottle to his lips. He barely registered its presence at first, then began taking in great gulps. He opened his eyes, and looked at his rescuers.

"How long have you been here like this?" asked Kim.

"I don't know at all..." he said in a croaking voice. "No idea... It went dark, then the sun came up again, then maybe went dark again?"

"My God! You've been out here for a couple of days?"

"Possibly... I'm not sure. I kept passing out, so I lost track of time... I can't feel my leg..."

"OK; hold tight there, and we'll get this stuff off you. What's your name?"

"Ricky... Thank you... Just take it real slow please..."

They lifted the rocks out of the way, and used their bare hands to gently sweep the soil off the unfortunate man. He yelled a few times as they moved the debris, and they apologised profusely. When they could see more of him, they quickly realised that he had a broken leg; it was lying bent at a rather unnatural angle.

"We're going to ring for an ambulance, Ricky," said Garth. "We think your leg is probably broken..."

"Oh, no, no! No...! I don't want an ambulance. I can't go to hospital! Can't you just fix me up a bit?"

"You're not thinking straight," replied Kim. "We can't mend a broken leg up here. It'll need an X-ray, and plastering. It would be difficult for us to even splint it so it's straight, up in this location!"

"Oh, no... But then the police will get involved, and I'll be in big trouble with the others..."

"Why? What others? You're not making much sense Ricky..."

"It doesn't matter... OK, just get me out of here please... Thank you."

They carried on trying to get all the dirt off the man, while Garth withdrew a small distance, and tried to make the call for an ambulance. Luckily, there was just enough signal here for the call to go through. It would probably be an hour-and-a-half before the ambulance reached the bottom of the track, and then a further 40 minutes for the paramedics to climb up to this spot. They had plenty of time, so they could try to make the casualty more comfortable, and get some more fluid and nourishment into him.

Calum volunteered to go back down to the truck and fetch Kim's medical kit, while Kim stayed with Ricky and kept him calm. Garth pulled Dana to one side, out of the victim's earshot, and shared some thoughts which were bothering him.

"I can't quite work out what's happening here, Dana. Something isn't right. This guy doesn't want to go to hospital, and he's worried about the police getting involved. He seems to be frightened of someone else too. What was he up to here? It's connected with this fence somehow; the area has obviously been fenced off for some unknown purpose. I wonder if we can drag it out of him?"

"Let Kim and me work on him," said Dana, "he might open up more to us girls."

Dana quietly explained Garth's thoughts to Kim, and they began trying to tease information out of the man, while getting him to take in more fluid, and eat an energy bar. He seemed very reluctant to talk, but was pleased to drink and eat. He was ravenous, and parched. The downside to his reviving was that it seemed to increase the pain he was feeling from his leg.

After a while, Calum returned with the medical kit, and Kim found some powerful painkillers for Ricky. She also cleaned some minor scrapes on his hands, but luckily, he did not seem to have any other obvious open wounds. But she had not looked at his leg yet.

"Right, Ricky, I'm going to look at your leg now. I'll have to cut your trouser leg open so I can see," she told him. "I am a paramedic, by the way..."

"OK; thank you..."

Kim set to work with the rather small pair of scissors from her medical kit, revealing the injured leg. It was not lying straight, so it was quite obviously broken, but fortunately there was no bone protruding through the skin anywhere. On the other hand, the whole limb was a horrible colour from the extensive bruising he had suffered.

"It looks like a fairly straightforward break, Ricky, but it's badly bruised as well. I can't really do anything more here on my own. But they'll fix you up in the hospital, don't worry."

Ricky just nodded assent.

There was nothing more to be done without specialised equipment, so they settled down to wait for the paramedics, and the stretcher they would bring. At least, the casualty's discomfort would have been numbed a little by the time they arrived on the scene to move him.

Garth decided on a slightly tougher line of questioning to try to get the man to talk, threatening to leave him alone to his fate if he didn't tell them what was going on. Ricky seemed to be living in great fear of reprisals by some party if the authorities became involved. Eventually, Garth softened his stance, and assured him that whatever was happening in this location was of no importance whatever to him and his three companions, who didn't even live in this region. It made no difference to them what Ricky had been up to, he told him. But he was still reluctant to say anything.

Eventually, after much persuasion, Ricky began to reveal to Kim some of the background to his presence at the site. The others gathered close to him again, and listened carefully to his story. It seemed that, beyond the crest which rose above them there was an extensive plateau area, and a meteorite had landed there some days earlier, at the same time as the one which struck Swellendam. Ricky had previously got to know a group of men who investigated meteorite strikes. They had learned that when a space-rock struck a deposit of graphite, the unimaginable shock pressures generated by the impact instantly created a layer of diamonds. It was common knowledge in geological circles that the huge Popigai impact crater in northern Siberia held the largest known deposit of diamonds on earth. Meteorite-formed diamonds were not gemstone grade, but they were still very valuable as industrial diamonds, and therefore quite sought after.

The gang Ricky was involved with moved quickly to locate new meteorite strike locations, and harvest whatever diamonds they could find. The practice was banned by law, the state having decided that all such new geological treasure-trove was government property. In the event, the impact crater above where they stood now had not yielded very much in the way of usable diamonds.

However, while they were searching for the crater, the gang had stumbled across the fenced-off area below the ridge.

Apparently, the area had been quietly screened off by the government archaeological services, because it had been discovered that this was the location of an ancient, pre-Apocalypse watering hole. The ground here was full of the skeletons of all kinds of animals, predators and prey, which had gathered here in large numbers to drink following the big meteorite strike. Many of them had been unable to feed normally as the dust fall-out settled all over the area. Then, when the water here had turned into a muddy sludge, the animals had been unable to drink sufficiently, and then they had collapsed and died in the mud. The dust and ash had covered the site, which had remained buried because of the topography here. Whereas much dust and ash had been gradually eroded away from higher ground by the wind over the centuries, this spot had remained immune to wind erosion, and so the skeletons had remained buried.

The gang had broken into the fenced site quite easily, and discovered a treasure that was even more valuable than the elusive diamonds. The trading of pre-Apocalypse animal remains was also forbidden by law, but there was a strong and active black market in operation, worldwide. Ricky had not been very happy about joining in with this plunder, but his group were small players, overseen by a ruthless gang of international criminals. He had had no option but to take part in the theft. It was a tragic loss to science. Government academics and scientists were trying to extract the DNA from the remains of species which were now extinct, or had at best two or three remaining individuals living in zoos. They were attempting to recreate the animals for posterity, to make a bio-diverse population which could eventually be reintroduced to the wild. But meanwhile, criminal gangs were stealing the skeletons for wealthy unscrupulous collectors all around the world.

Ricky's gang had visited the site several times, always at night, digging out entire skeletons of large iconic animals, such as tigers and lions. On their last visit, they had been hard at work when a portion of the escarpment had suddenly detached itself from the hill, and overrun the area. His companions had fled for their lives, leaving him for dead.

Having described his involvement, Ricky could see the distaste written all over the faces of his rescuers.

"I didn't do this as a career choice you know..." he told them. "I had no option. I had lost my job and my family home, because of unscrupulous builders and the incompetence and lethargy of officialdom! With my wife and two children, we live in a one-bedroom studio flat now, instead of the big home we used to have..."

"But what about your wife, Ricky? Don't you have a phone on you that you could have used to call for help, and let her know what had happened to you? She must be worried sick!" said Kim.

"No, we didn't bring phones with us, because their exact location can be traced. We were told that on no account were we to bring one. These guys would have just about killed us if they had found a phone on one of us... They're totally ruthless."

"So what happened to you to make you take up this activity?" asked Garth.

Ricky took another long swig of water before answering.

"Just a few months ago, with my family, we were living in a nice, brand new place on the southern edge of Swellendam, built by the local authority. We had our shop on the ground floor, and home above. It had a nice big garden at the back, and outbuildings too. It was newly-built, all beautiful. We sold high-class women's clothing. The first thing that happened was the earthquake last year. Big cracks appeared in the building, which was odd, because they were all supposed to be earthquake-proof. It was one of a row, all new, all purpose-built. They all had the same problem, caused by someone taking short-cuts in the construction... So suddenly, the insurance company says they're increasing our premiums, because the buildings are not deemed safe. They multiplied the figure by a factor of ten! We could barely afford it; it was taking nearly all our earnings just to pay them, but you have to have insurance, by law... The business was newly-established, and hadn't really got going yet.

Then the big one hit, just a few months back... The place just about collapsed around our ears! Luckily, none of us was killed, but my youngest daughter had her arm and one hip broken. She's only five! She's the sweetest little thing. My wife was hit on the head by something. She still has double-vision sometimes. Some of the other houses in the row were still standing, but looked really dangerous. The authorities made everyone get out immediately. We'd already had to move in with my in-laws, because our building had completely fallen down. They allocated us this one-bedroom flat, with no garden, no view, nothing... We lost everything – job, home, personal stuff... All our old family photographs and archive on our computers, clothes... All the stock ruined... Then, the insurance company says they're not paying out, because the building was constructed negligently! There's a fight going on between them and the local authority, and our lawyers tell us it could take three years to settle. In the meantime, we're living in this rabbit-hutch, and we've got nothing but the four walls around us. We're living on hand-outs..."

"Then I met these guys at a football match. They said they had some well-paid work they could offer, and were looking for another fit man like me to join their crew. The only thing was, it was night work... Like a sucker, I fell for it. But there was just nothing else going. There's quite a lot of unemployment down here right now..."

The others had been listening quietly. Ricky's tale was horrifying. They saw tears forming in his eyes, and looked away from him, feeling embarrassed. There was a long pause while they digested what he had said, then Garth spoke quietly.

"God, Ricky, that really sucks... I'm really sorry. I don't quite know what to say... But I'll tell you this: none of us here will say a word about what you've been doing, if that's what you want. I don't know if it will make any difference though. I'm afraid that someone may ask how you came to be injured up here..."

"Yeah, I know, I'm stuffed really... Thanks for for rescuing me, and for hearing me out. I'll just have to live with the consequences, I suppose. I'm just a bit scared of the gangsters behind all this... They don't take kindly to people revealing their little secrets... What a mess... Oh, shit! This leg hurts!"

"Try to keep still Ricky" said Kim, laying her hand on his arm. "You've been getting worked up, and wriggling around, which doesn't help..."

"The paramedics should get here pretty soon now," said Calum. "They'll probably give you a shot of something for the pain before moving you."

"That'd be good."

Right on cue, they heard the paramedics calling to them from down the path a little way.

"Up here!" Dana and Garth called back in unison, standing tall and waving.

The two medics appeared, two fit-looking young men clad in their green scrubs, one of them carrying a folded lightweight stretcher. Kim went over to meet them, and described the casualty's injuries and general state of health. They immediately set to work, talking to Ricky to establish his state of mind as well as physical condition, and administering a pain-killing injection. They allowed this to act for a minute or two before fitting a temporary splint to the broken limb, and attempting to move the man onto the stretcher. The six of them all helped to lift Ricky in one swift movement, speeding the operation considerably. The next problem was how to carry the casualty all the way back down to the road without hurting him. It was not easy, with the considerable slope the path took on at times, but the four men each took a corner of the stretcher, lightening the load for them all.

Dana and Kim followed on behind, discussing the situation, and whether there was anything they could do to help Ricky and his family. They had managed to get him to remember his wife's phone number, and had called her while the others set off slowly down the path. Unsurprisingly, she had been distraught, but calmed down gradually as they explained that Ricky had had an accident through no fault of his own, and was now being taken to hospital with a suspected broken leg. They asked for her address, and promised to go and visit her later in the day, and maybe accompany her to the hospital.

The four friends had discussed whether to pretend that Ricky was hiking with them when he had had a fall, but this would not have washed with the paramedics, who could tell from the casualty's state that he had been lying unattended for some considerable time, and was suffering from dehydration on top of his injuries. Kim knew from her own experience that questions were usually asked about the cause of accidents and injuries, and feared that it could be tricky to explain this one away. Ricky could claim that he had been out hiking on his own, but how had he reached the site? It was miles from anywhere, and he had no vehicle nearby. It all depended how keen anyone was to discover the real reason for the man's presence at this remote location. It was just conceivable that no-one would show any interest; they would just have to wait and see... The crime scene – the ancient former water-hole, was now covered in a great pile of rocks and soil, so it would be a long time before the archaeological services realised that someone had been plundering the site. The other problem was the real criminals behind the operation. Would they be taking an interest in Ricky now, or would they just forget about him? It was an uncomfortable situation...

Eventually, the stretcher-bearers reached the road, having stopped three times to take a short rest. The paramedics loaded Ricky into the ambulance, and the four friends watched it drive off, having assured Ricky that they would come and visit him in the hospital, later on. They stood quietly for a while by the truck, reflecting on the strange turn of events. They had all felt uplifted and carefree earlier on, but now the spell had been broken.

"I think I want to go home..." said Kim finally.

"I know, Kim," said Dana. "Let's just go and see Ricky's wife, and then we'll try and figure out how we're going to get back north. What do you say, guys?"

Garth and Calum nodded assent.

***

They drove back to Swellendam, hitting the suburbs in late afternoon, and made their way to the block of flats where Ricky and his family now lived. The area was a mixed development of flats of various sizes, with numerous starter-homes designed for single people, and ground-floor flats for more elderly residents. There was a slightly uncared-for appearance to the buildings. They found the right block and parked. Dana wondered whether it was a good idea for them all to turn up together, but they decided that it would take too long to drop off half the party back at their hotel, and that Ricky's wife might be dealing with cooking and bath-time for the children later, so it would be better for them to all go now. They would see how Melania – Ricky's wife – seemed, and act accordingly. Garth and Calum held back a bit, while Kim and Dana rang the doorbell at Ricky's front door. They heard a slightly raised voice, and saw a woman's silhouette moving through the frosted glass of the door. Melania opened the door a crack, and said hello in a questioning way.

"Hello Melania," said Kim, "I spoke to you earlier. My name is Kim, and this is Dana. We found Ricky this morning, and gave him first aid treatment."

Melania opened the door wider, and caught sight of Garth and Calum, clearly looking frightened by this sudden deputation arriving at her flat. There was a slightly far-away look in her eyes.

"It's OK, this is Calum and Garth, they're our husbands. We won't all come in if it's not convenient."

She quickly recovered her poise. "Well, there isn't room for you all to sit down, but you can come in if you like..."

Melania showed them in to a small living room, which had a kitchen in one corner. Two little girls were sitting on cushions on the floor, looking at a television with the sound muted. They looked round at the visitors curiously, without smiling. Melania motioned to Kim and Dana to sit on the sofa, while she sat down on the one armchair. Garth and Calum stood to one side, feeling slightly awkward.

"Ricky should be getting treated by now," said Kim. "We saw him off in the ambulance just over an hour ago. We think he has a fractured femur."

Tears came to Melania's eyes, and began to run down her cheeks. Kim quickly moved over and crouched in front of her, taking one of her hands.

"He'll be OK. Obviously it will take a while for him to mend, but he'll be all right. We could take you to the hospital later, if you like. One of the guys could take you, and Dana and I could baby-sit the girls, if you like?"

"My parents can come over, so there's no need, thank you. But where did this happen, and how come Ricky was left on his own?"

Kim and Dana explained how Ricky had come to be abandoned at the site of the landslide. Melania seemed to know about the illicit diamond-mining operations. They did not mention the bone digging, guessing that this might be one element too many for the woman to take in at this time. It might be better if she was unaware of it anyway. After a while, Melania seemed relieved to have these young strangers to speak to, and began describing the events of the previous months, confirming everything that Ricky had said about the loss of their previous home and their sudden financial difficulties. But she assured them that her parents would come round later, and that her father would take her to the hospital while her mother looked after the children. Kim apologised for having had to break the bad news to her, and said she would telephone the next day to find out how they were all doing. The four companions bade their good byes, and returned to the truck.

"Well, that's just dandy, isn't it..." said Garth, looking depressed. "I can't see what we can do to help the poor woman..."

"No... I feel a bit helpless," agreed Dana.

"There must be so much of this going on around here just now," said Kim. "What with the earthquake casualties and the unemployment situation... I don't think that we can help really. We've done our first aid bit, and now we need to go back home before we get thrown out of our jobs too..."

***

The foursome visited Ricky in the hospital the next morning. He was about to be discharged, having been rehydrated, and fed, and had his leg plastered. They could hardly believe how much better he looked, and how positive he sounded. He was a tough character. There had been no awkward questions so far about his accident, and he was hopeful now that he would be forgotten about. His father-in-law had heard of some jobs starting up in a couple of months, which might just coincide with Ricky's leg being healed. There was a glimmer of optimism for the future. Garth left a business card with him, and asked him to let them know how his recovery went, and what happened about their home.

SEVENTEEN

Kim had been worrying about the return journey north. She did not relish the idea of another eight day drive across the vast desert lands. In any case, how would four of them manage in the truck? It had not been too uncomfortable for two of them to sleep across the bench seats, but four was a different matter. Would two of them be able to lie down in the cargo area, or would it be too crowded with the necessary equipment and supplies? She thought that it was probably too short anyway. She kept thinking about Melania and her daughters, but could not think of a way to help them. Her mind was clogged with concerns, and she could not see a solution.

In the end, strings were pulled by the Swellendam authorities. In recognition of the volunteers' sterling efforts, and after consultation with Garth and Dana, two precious seats had been allocated on a flight between Mandela and Laxberg, and these had been promised to Kim and Calum. Garth and Dana were not fazed by the idea of the eight-day return drive; in fact, Garth was quite looking forward to it.

The two couples enjoyed each other's company for another three days, two of which were spent back in Mandela, staying at Maxine and Trevor's guest-house. The latter welcomed the foursome with open arms, and cracked open a bottle of bubbly to celebrate their return to Mandela.

On their last day, Dana and Garth accompanied Kim and Calum to the city-centre airport terminal building, from where buses left at regular intervals to take passengers out to the airport itself. They sat together as they waited, then there were tearful goodbyes, but also heartfelt promises to stay in touch.

"You're not going to keep me away!" Dana said to Kim. "I'll be wanting to know how this baby is growing, and I'll be third in line to hold him – after Calum and your mum, understood?"

"OK Dana. I'll put you on the list. I'm going to miss you, but not for long, do you hear? Come and see us soon. And for God's sake, please be careful on your return journey! Let me know the minute you're back. Thank you for everything.."

"What are you thanking me for? I can't imagine what would have happened to me if you hadn't been there for me... We'll be careful... I think Garth wants to see if he can find any diamonds in the craters in Crater Plain. But I'll try and restrain him if I can!"

"Bring a couple back for us, but don't get arrested!"

They waved each other off, and Calum and Kim climbed aboard the bus.

***

Early the next day, Dana and Garth set off for Dontsane, to go and visit his parents. She had been in touch with her superiors at the university, and had managed to negotiate some more time off, unpaid. Garth was due some leave, so decided to make full use of it now. They finally made it back to Laxberg two full weeks later. The return journey had gone quite smoothly. Newly freed from anxieties, they had enjoyed the trip and all its strange sights.

EIGHTEEN

Dana and Garth had greatly enjoyed their stay with his parents. While Garth had managed to visit them briefly on a number of occasions in the last three years, thanks to his work in the south, Dana had not seen them in quite a while. They were a lovely, easy-going couple, and had been very welcoming towards her. The four of them had enjoyed a couple of outings to a local beach, with lavish al-fresco lunches, and they felt more refreshed and relaxed than for a long time. It was a welcome break after the drama of the previous couple of weeks. But they had to face the inevitable return to work, and the very long trek home. Another tearful departure ensued, and then they were on their way, just the two of them.

From Dontsane, they had to take the H10 highway, which headed north-west, and would finally intersect with the north-bound H2 after some 1,400 kilometres. It was an epic journey across magnificent scenery, with broad tracts of farmland initially, and a constant backdrop of distant mountains. But then they were crossing the seemingly endless veldt, a vast empty plateau, sometimes lush and green, although treeless, elsewhere more arid, with bare patches of the red earth showing through between clumps of thinner vegetation. The traffic was light, and they were enjoying the feeling of embarking on an adventure together, just the two of them, and the anticipation of new sights and sensations shared. After a long day's driving, they stopped overnight at a remote and inexpensive motel, which would be their last comfortable night for another week.

The next morning, they rejoined the H10, still crossing the veldt. By midday, they were travelling parallel to a big river, and there were broad tracts of farmland on either side, making use of the water to irrigate the crops. Ranges of mountains still formed a backdrop on either side. After a couple of hours of following the river's course, the highway left it behind, still heading north-west. There were only about three hundred kilometres to go now, before they hit the H2. The endless ribbon of tarmac unravelled beneath them, inducing a pleasant torpor in the travellers. The truck's lane-assist constantly monitored their course, ensuring that the driver did not fall asleep and drive off into the scenery.

They were rudely awakened from their reverie by an unexpected barrier, stretching completely across the road just after a small intersection, accompanied by a large "road closed ahead" sign. A diversion sign indicated that they had to take a small road off to the right, which would presumably take them back to the H10 a bit further ahead.

"I wonder what this is about," said Garth. "There was no warning about it on the online map service..."

"I expect it's just road-works," said Dana.

"Seems odd to divert traffic so far around the works though..." replied Garth. "Anyway, we don't have any other option."

They turned down the side road, which took them two or three kilometres in the wrong direction, before they arrived at a crossroads, where diversion signs indicated that they should turn left. At least they were now travelling in roughly the right direction again, on a small road parallel to the H10. Five kilometres on, they passed a small turning to the left, but diversion signs insisted that they should continue straight ahead for the time being. The small road seemed to be gradually converging back towards the main road. Not long after the small side turning, they reached a high point in the land which gave them a view across to the left, towards where they thought the H10 should lie. Suddenly, they caught sight of major activity over to their left, and slowed down to try and see what was happening. There seemed to be a small impact crater over there, and several very large vehicles; a low-loader lorry maybe, and a crane or two. Nothing that looked like typical road-laying machinery though.

Garth stopped the truck, and tried to understand what was going on at the main highway. Then he abruptly made a three-point turn in the road, and turned back towards the small side turning they had just passed.

"Oh, Garth... For crying out loud! What are you doing?" complained Dana. "We've got days of driving ahead of us, and now you're doubling back in the wrong direction!"

"It's only going to take five minutes... I just want to see what's happening over there. It's hardly going to delay us..."

Dana felt annoyed, but could not summon the will to argue. They soon arrived back at the small side-turning, and Garth turned right into it, driving around the diversion arrow sign planted in the middle of the road. There soon followed two further signs, marked "ROAD CLOSED AHEAD" and "STRICTLY NO ADMITTANCE". Garth had to drive onto the verge to go around these signs, while Dana squirmed in her seat, feeling very uneasy.

"You're going to get us into big trouble here, Garth! What's the point?"

"Oh, come on, Dana, I just want a quick look. We'll turn back in five minutes, OK?"

Dana said nothing. They carried on, until they came to a point that was slightly elevated, and from which they had a commanding view of the work going on on the main highway, which lay maybe 500 metres away. Garth stopped the truck at a spot where it would be concealed to anyone on the H2 by a small ridge. He climbed out, taking his phone with him, as well as pair of compact field glasses. After a short delay, Dana got out of the truck too, and followed him reluctantly. They squatted close to the top of the ridge, and peered across towards the activity below.

Just as they had reached their vantage point, they saw a large mobile crane begin to lift a large and very heavy looking object out of a small crater. A low-loader lorry stood close by, ready to receive whatever it was. The area seemed to be teeming with military personnel, most just standing around watching the operation, and many of them armed. The object slowly came up into view above the rim of the crater. It looked like some kind of aircraft, possibly, although nothing recognisable, and it did not seem to have wings. Garth looked through his binoculars. The object looked remarkably undamaged, considering the crater-burrowing force with which it must have struck the ground.

"What the hell is that?" he asked Dana. "It's not an aircraft, that's for sure..."

Dana's reticence had disappeared; she was now equally transfixed by the activity unfolding in front of them.

"I can't imagine... Is it a missile of some sort, or a space-craft?"

"But no-one's doing any space missions, are they?"

"Not that I've heard... Could it be an ancient satellite that's come back down to earth?"

"I thought that they burned up when they hit the atmosphere..." replied Garth.

"It's huge too!" said Dana.

"That thing was never made on earth," Garth suddenly pronounced. "Look at it – it's dug a crater in the ground, but it looks completely unmarked! The side of it is polished and shiny..."

"Let me look through the binoculars please," asked Dana. Garth handed the glasses over, and opened his phone. He clipped a little telephoto lens to the device, and started taking photographs of the scene and the object.

"I could be wrong I suppose, but I'd swear that that object is an alien craft!" Garth said, as he zoomed in on the photos he had just taken. "It's incredible..."

"I think you're right," agreed Dana. "It doesn't look like anything I've ever seen, or any object I've ever seen a photograph of... It's a strange shape..."

"And that opens up a whole lot of other questions... Like, what was it doing, and how did it come to crash-land here, and so on..."

By now, the strange object was in complete view, suspended in mid-air above the low-loader, and beginning to be lowered. It was wedge-shaped, with one quite pointed end, and a smooth, very highly polished 'hull'. There seemed to be a door-sized hatch on the side, but with very tight shut lines which were quite hard to discern. As the object swivelled on its straps, Garth became aware of markings on its flank, like writing or numerals, but not in any kind of recognisable language or script.

"What does that say on its side, Dana?" he asked.

"They're just kind of hieroglyphics," she answered. "That's no language I've ever come across..."

"My God, this is mind-blowing!" said Garth.

They were suddenly startled by a sound from behind them. They looked round, to see three big men in military uniforms striding very quietly towards them from a four-wheel-drive all-terrain vehicle, which had parked 25 metres behind their truck. They had been so engrossed by the alien craft and distracted by the sounds of the recovery operation, that they had not heard the other vehicle approach.

"Stay exactly where you are!" said the nearest of the three men. The newcomers came closer. They were Self-Defence Force personnel; one had sergeant's stripes, another was a corporal, and the third had no visible markings. They were all armed with automatic pistols and batons in holsters. The sergeant asked Garth and Dana to stand up, and not to make any sudden moves.

"What are you doing here?" asked the sergeant.

"We just turned off the main road to see what's going on here..." answered Garth.

"You passed three signs which quite clearly state that this road is out of bounds!" said the sergeant. "Do you have any I.D.?"

"In the truck, yes. Do you want me to get it?"

"You fetch it please," he said, pointing at Dana. The third soldier accompanied her to the truck, watching her very closely as she fumbled in the glove-box for their documents. She handed their identity cards over to the soldier, who glanced at them, then took them to his superior. The sergeant and the corporal examined the documents together.

"Mister Garth Mirey," said the corporal, "from Laxberg. Wait a minute, I recognise you. Sergeant, this is the 'hero' who was digging people out of the rubble in Swellendam a couple of weeks ago." He spoke in a sneering tone of voice, with a smirk on his face.

"Well, Mr Mirey, it's so good of you to come all the way from Laxberg to rescue us poor helpless southerners," said the sergeant, in a mocking tone. "But what business do you have, poking your nose into this area?"

"Well, firstly I'm a southerner myself," replied Garth, "although I live in Laxberg now, I'm from Dontsane. We were just passing, and just happened to notice your operation there..."

"Except that you didn't pass it. You decided to come and investigate, despite the obvious road closure and the multiple signs!"

"Well, I didn't see that we were doing any harm... We're just passing through, and there seemed to be something unusual going on..."

"Right. Well, the road was closed for a reason; for the public's protection," said the sergeant. "Now, did you take any photographs? I notice that you have your phone there, with a telephoto lens."

"I might have taken a couple of shots, yes..." answered Garth.

"Give it to me please," said the sergeant, holding out his hand. Garth handed over his phone. The corporal pulled a strange-looking small device from a bag he was carrying. It looked a bit like a hot-glue gun or a small hair dryer, with multiple buttons and a trigger. He pointed the gadget at Garth's phone and pulled the trigger. To Dana and

Garth's amazement, his locked phone's screen instantly came to life, and was displaying the most recently-taken photos. The man touched a button on the device and pulled the trigger again. The photographs instantly disappeared from the phone's screen. *How on earth did that happen?* - thought Garth.

"There you are," the sergeant said to Garth, handing back his phone. "It's unharmed. And you, Miss? Did you take any photographs with any other device? I will need to check."

"No," said Dana. "My phone is still in the truck... Did you want to see it?"

"Yes please."

Dana went back to the truck, and brought back her phone, the third soldier shadowing her closely again. She had nothing to hide. The sergeant and corporal went through the same procedure again, but seemed satisfied, and did not appear to delete anything from her phone.

"So where are you people heading now?" asked the sergeant.

"We're on our way back to Laxberg," said Dana.

"Laxberg?" repeated the sergeant, sounding totally incredulous. "That's a trip and a half! So you had so much time on your hands that you just thought you'd check out the road-works here?"

"My husband was intrigued..." said Dana. "We didn't think we were doing anything wrong..."

"Well, as I said, the road is closed for a reason, and this is a Restricted Place," said the sergeant. "Now, I suggest that you get back in your truck, and continue on your journey immediately..."

"OK," said Garth. "We weren't wanting to cause any trouble. We'll get on our way. But, before we go, can you just confirm to us that that is an alien craft over there?"

The sergeant and corporal began to look very irritated.

"No. Just get on your way, Mister Mirey!"

"And do not stop within sixty kilometres of this point," added the corporal. "We are tracking all vehicles by radar, so if you stop again, we will come and investigate. Got that?"

"We're going right now," said Dana, pulling Garth's arm towards their truck.

Garth got behind the wheel of the truck, and Dana got into the front passenger seat. He started up, and made a multi-point turn in the narrow road, then set off, passing the soldiers' vehicle. Garth could see in the rear-view mirror that the soldiers were watching them drive away. He and Dana sat quietly in their seats, feeling chastised and shaken. They passed the road closure signs, and rejoined the road parallel to the H10, before speaking another word.

"Well, what did you make of that?" Garth asked.

"My God, I'm freaked out!" answered Dana. "Those guys were deeply unpleasant. What is it that makes men in uniform become so arrogant and self-important?"

"I know... Look, I'm sorry that all that happened. I shouldn't have stopped, I know..."

"Well, maybe not, but those guys' reaction was totally out of proportion! And now of course, I'm wondering all the more what it is they're trying to cover up, and why? And then, if they really didn't want anyone driving down that road, why didn't they block it off properly? Like at the main road where we had to turn off. It doesn't make sense!"

"No... It's typical warped military thinking. They think they're superior to the ordinary public, when it's the public that pays for them in the first place."

"But I'll tell you something, Garth: everything is suddenly looking a whole lot clearer to me."

"What do you mean?"

"Well, when Kim and I arrived in Mandela, we were just told there had been some meteorite strikes beyond the normal season, and further south than usual. It seemed a bit lame, as an excuse to close the H2 for weeks on end, and the comms black-out."

"That wasn't entirely untrue... After all, the strike on Swellendam was a long way south, and then there was the one near where Ricky was digging up the bones..."

"Yes, but I think those were just useful scapegoats. The real reason they closed the highway for so long is because of this alien craft! They probably didn't dare go too close to it for ages... They would have been sitting at a distance, just watching it, for some time."

"And what if it's not the only one?" asked Garth. "Maybe there were one or more others that landed in the area. You can see why that would have made the military all jumpy!"

"I wouldn't be surprised if there were others. But then, what's happened to the occupants? Did they survive the crash-landing, or did it kill them all? Or is that thing remotely operated, or even robotic?"

"I don't suppose we'll ever know... And now, Sergeant Smart-Ass there has deleted all the photos I took, so we have no evidence at all, and no-one is going to believe a word of this if we tell them..."

"No... It's weird how those in authority behave with something unusual like this. They always seem to want to cover it up, and deny its existence..."

"True enough... I wonder what they're going to do with that thing now? I suppose they'll try to open it up, and analyse the technology."

"Well, the best of luck with that... I don't think it will give up its secrets lightly. And, what if its owners come down, and say they want their space-craft back? I can't imagine they would take 'no' for an answer!"

"Right. It hardly bears thinking about..."

"Do you think that there's any connection between that vehicle and the meteorite strikes?"

"I can't quite see it... No, I think the meteorites are just a thing of their own. They've been coming down for years now, and I've never heard the slightest hint of extra-terrestrials visiting."

"Hmmm." Dana was quiet for a while, thinking about all the historical reports of alleged alien visitations, going back through centuries. One in particular seemed significant, though still unexplained.

" I seem to remember reading about UFOs crash-landing in the desert centuries ago, pre-Apocalypse, in North America I think. The name Roswell rings a bell..."

"And what happened there?"

"Well, it's never been officially admitted to, but there were stories of this craft crashing down, and there were supposedly aliens who survived the accident, or at the least, they found bodies. They were taken to a military research facility nearby, and then it all went quiet..."

"Their friends didn't come immediately to exact revenge then?"

"Not that I'm aware of, no."

"So this craft is not likely to be related to that incident, after all this time..."

"It's very unlikely, I suppose. But who knows? It's so frustrating, because we might never hear anything more about what we've just seen..."

"Either that, or else there will suddenly be an invasion armada!"

***

NINETEEN

Seven days after they had left his parents' home in Dontsane, Garth and Dana had passed the Devil's Fingers, driving northwards. Then they had arrived at the place on the H2 highway where the impact crater had blocked the road. They reached it in late afternoon, to find that work was well in hand to create the new diversion of the road around the crater. There was a temporary surface, which was a bit rough, and temporary barriers everywhere to direct the traffic. There was an encampment nearby for the road workers, with large trailer-houses and a portable office building. Huge road-laying machines and excavators stood idle, because work had ended for the day. The traffic was very light, as the road had not been re-opened long, and commerce between south and north had not fully resumed yet.

Dana had told Garth about this place, and he had been thinking about it from time to time, and had decided to stop and take a look at the crater when they reached it. And so now, finding few other vehicles around, Garth drove off the tarmac and onto the hard shoulder of the road. He had a magnetic amber flashing light in the truck for his work, and when he got out of the truck, he attached this to the roof of the vehicle and turned it on. He reached for a small cloth bag, which contained a little hammer and a trowel. He donned his hard hat, so that to any casual passer-by, he looked like one of the roadwork crew, working late. Donna joined him as he scrambled up the side of the crater, stopping at the rim to survey the surroundings. She felt a bit uneasy about this second bout of trespassing, but Garth was so head-strong; she knew that she could not stop him from doing what he wanted. They could see for miles all around from up there. There was nobody around to ask them what they were doing, and certainly no military.

Garth headed for the centre of the crater. Most of the circular-shaped depression's surface was quite smooth, but a fairly large boulder sat at the centre, surrounded by rocky rubble. It was clear that the site had been investigated previously. There were signs of digging around the base of the big boulder, and most of the large rocks around the largest one had been turned over and rolled aside. It was hardly surprising, but disappointing. Nevertheless, Garth pulled his trowel out of the bag, and began poking around the rocks, and the base of the large rock. There were some small, slightly sparkling surfaces there, but they were dirty and insignificant. Not that raw rough diamonds were particularly spectacular in appearance; they tended to appear rather grey before being polished. There were signs that the central boulder's surface had begun cracking and peeling away like a big onion as it cooled following the impact. Flattish fragments of rock were lying around here and there. Garth tapped at the rock close to its base, and fragments fell away, but revealed nothing but more rock. It was a waste of time... There might be diamonds beneath the boulder, but it would take a mechanical digger to turn this one over.

"I think we're a bit late coming to this," he said to Dana. "The site has been well and truly plundered!"

"Yes, it looks that way..." agreed Dana.

Garth strolled casually around the central area, fascinated by the variety of different colours displayed on the smaller rocks. Then he ambled across toward the far side of the crater. He noticed a small triangular shard poking up out of the slope of the crater wall, and tried to pull it up. It was more resistant than he had expected; it must be larger than he thought. He picked around it gently with his trowel, and soon the shard came free. It was an arc-shaped, dished fragment, about twenty to twenty-five centimetres across, rather like a tiara in form and size, and covered in dust. He blew the dirt off the inner side, and turned it over to clean the outer surface. Suddenly, Garth was looking at a surface evenly studded with clear sparkling crystals, with a slightly purple tinge. He wiped a small area with his thumb, and the crystals flashed a rainbow of coloured glints in the last rays of sunlight. He stood looking at the object for a moment, totally dumb-struck. He quickly realised that it was a segment of an amethyst geode, which had coincidentally come to be unearthed by the impact. Not diamonds, unfortunately... He called to Dana.

"Hey, Dana, come and look at this!"

She walked over to him, and he raised the object above her head with his two hands.

"A tiara for my beautiful princess!"

TWENTY

Five months later, Garth was surprised when he received an email from Ricky. After his discharge from the hospital, he had received a visit from a couple of policemen, who wanted to know more about the circumstances of his injury at the remote location where he had been found. The state archaeological services had cleared some of the spoil from the site where they were excavating bones, and discovered that the ancient animal grave had been plundered. The police had become involved, and had learned about Ricky's injury at the location. They suspected that he was part of a gang involved in finding and smuggling animal skeletons. Ricky was too basically honest to attempt to conceal his involvement, and his fear of the gangsters was immediately apparent to the police. In return for a promise of protection, he disclosed all the information that he knew about the crime overlords. Although this was relatively little, he had been able to recall some vehicle registration numbers and a few other details, which he had made a careful mental note of just in case of such an eventuality. This had led to some of the big players being identified and arrested, and to the recovery of some of the bones. Many others had unfortunately disappeared without trace. Ricky and his family had been rehoused in a different area, and he had started a new job.

TWENTY-ONE

One month after their return to Laxberg, Dana and Garth were at home, watching the evening television news. There was a report from Southern Province about an exciting archaeological find near the town of Voolsdrift. A small meteorite had come down during the earlier 'season', very close to the main H2 highway. When the site was examined, it emerged that a number of large pre-Apocalypse animal skeletons had been unearthed. It was believed that the meteorite had accidentally uncovered a former watering-hole. There followed a report from the channel's local correspondent, with video footage of the scene from various angles, including close-ups of the skeleton of a big cat being carefully uncovered from the soil. Something about the surroundings struck Garth suddenly.

"Wait a minute," he exclaimed, "isn't that the place where we saw the space-craft being recovered? Wind it back a bit, Dana…"

Dana stopped the live feed, and wound it back to the wide view of the excavation scene.

"That first shot is taken from where we stopped to watch the recovery operation!" she said. "I'm sure of it!"

"Right! So what's going on there? Is this an elaborate cover-up? Press 'play' again…"

They watched the whole piece again.

"I'm not terribly convinced," said Garth. "They've shown one skeleton, or maybe even just part of one. It hardly amounts to a major archaeological find, does it? And then, do you think the topography of the area looks plausible for a water-hole?"

"I'm not sure on that. I suppose that the area could have changed a bit in two thousand years or so. But, as you say, it does smack a bit of deliberate obfuscation. Needless to say, there's no mention of alien space-craft!"

"No. You know, I can't believe that we were the only ones to notice the recovery operation that was going on. I mean, there was a fair bit of traffic going along that road in the two directions, and we went along that raised section, from which you could clearly see something going on. Something that didn't seem to be involving road-laying equipment. They don't use big cranes to lay tarmac..."

"True. But how would you find out if anyone else noticed what was happening? And without getting into trouble with the authorities..."

"I'm not sure... But I think that I might get in touch with the news agencies down there. I can tell them what we saw, and maybe find out if they've had any other reports on similar lines."

"Well, I suppose you can ask. But I'm a bit scared of those guys who found us back there..."

"What are they going to do? They didn't tell us to keep quiet about we saw. They just denied anything unusual was going on, and deleted my photos. I can't see that it's worth their while to come and hassle us. If they just ignore us, then we look like cranks, which is probably how they want to play it..."

A day or two later, after a little research, Garth emailed the Southern Times and the Southern Argus, describing the recovery operation he and Dana had seen. A reporter from each of the news agencies expressed great interest, and a short exchange of emails followed. It turned out that a number of people had seen what Dana and Garth had witnessed, and they were anxious to know more. A prominent local Member of Parliament had been one of the passers-by to witness the operation, and he had begun asking questions at a high level. He was not satisfied with being fobbed off, and was demanding an explanation. He had travelled back to the site, and observed the so-called archaeological dig, and was convinced that it was a sham. The story was gaining traction in the news media.

Garth received an email from the M.P., asking for full details of what he had seen, and the military's actions. The man was as intrigued by the incident as Garth was, and could not see any logical reason for a government cover-up. He had gathered more than twenty accounts from law-abiding citizens, all describing the sight of a mysterious unidentifiable object being transported from the crash site.

The straw that broke the camel's back was the leaking by persons unknown of official reports describing the alien craft and its recovery. Copies of these were sent directly to the investigating M.P., who forwarded them to the Press. The authorities could no longer carry on with the denials, and were obliged to issue belated press releases.

Garth began to receive requests for interviews from news agencies and magazines. He was slightly fearful of repercussions from the military bodies down south, particularly in view of the fact that he might well be sent on work assignments there again in the future. But he reasoned that the story was now fully in the public domain. Also, a notable politician was aware of his position, and he was unlikely to allow victimisation of a member of the public to go by unpunished.

The clamour for information about the crashed space-craft grew and grew, with the public wanting as much detail as possible, and scientists worldwide demanding access to the alien vehicles. Before long it became apparent that the 'Voolsdrift Incident' was one of the most significant and extraordinary events of the post-Apocalypse era.

TWENTY-TWO

Six and a half months after her return home, Kim woke up early one morning, after a somewhat fitful night. Her bump was huge now, and it was difficult for her to find a comfortable position to sleep. She opened the curtains, revealing a beautiful, orange-streaked dawn sky. The sun was just breaking the horizon in the south-east. Then she noticed that, due east, three small pink clouds were hanging in front of the orange back-drop, almost touching each other, so that they formed a kind of heart shape. Kim suddenly remembered the words spoken to her by Miriam, a few months earlier, in the back of the ambulance. Just then, her waters broke.

*Excerpt from **A History of the Modern World** - 2nd edition – 1993 Post-Apocalypse*

Michael Olinsson, Professor of Modern History, University of Laxberg

©Laxberg University Press, 1993PA

"In 1992PA, information leaked out from government sources in Mandela, Southern Province, that two alien space-vehicles had been discovered in a region approximately 650 kilometres north of Mandela. The two craft, identical in design, appeared to have accidentally crash-landed in the veldt, close to the town of Voolsdrift. Following an initial attempt at stifling information, public interest peaked to such a level that the government was obliged to issue a statement about the incident, and eventually official press releases were issued describing the investigations and analysis of the devices.

The craft had evidently impacted the surface at high speed, resulting in the formation of impact craters some thirty metres in diameter, with a depth of between two and three metres. Curiously, neither vehicle appeared to be in any way externally damaged by the impact.

The two space-craft were initially kept under close observation by the military for a period of seven days, during which no movement or activity was detected. They were then recovered from the crash sites, and taken to Air Force workshops near Mandela, where extensive examinations began.

After entry to the craft had been forced, with great difficulty, it became apparent that these were unmanned vehicles, although they were each fitted with seats for four occupants. It is not known whether there were occupants at the time prior to impact, and whether they might have somehow ejected safely from the craft before they crashed, or otherwise fled the scene. The seats and other internal fittings suggest that the erstwhile occupants would be of a very similar size to humans.

The space-crafts' method of propulsion would appear to belong to a technology beyond our current understanding, despite our finest minds attempting to fathom its secrets. The sophisticated construction of the craft has elicited enormous interest in the scientific community. A number of metallic alloys and other synthetic plastic materials unknown on Earth have been discovered, all having the most remarkable properties, such as previously unattainably high melting points, and prodigious tensile strength.

Curiously, there have been no further landings of similar craft observed, and there seems to have been no attempt at recovery of the craft by their owners. This draws a parallel with information latterly claimed about an alleged similar incident in New Mexico, (former United States), which was reported in 1947AD - (86BA).

The main, and astonishing deduction to be made from the new incidents is that mankind now has irrefutable proof of the existence of a technologically sophisticated alien civilisation on another world. This knowledge has been sought for centuries by generations of astronomers and other scientists. It is frustrating that the aliens themselves remain elusive, and that there seems to be no indication of whether or if we will ever be able to make contact with them."

Acknowledgments

My grateful thanks to my wife, Ann, and our daughter, Amy, for proof-reading, and for making valuable suggestions to improve the plot-line of this tale.

If you are intrigued by the images of Abyssworld in this book, you can find many more in the the illustrated book dedicated to the series:

The Abyssworld
Drawings, Watercolours and Oil Paintings by
Nebbid Werdna

ISBN - 978-0-9956254-1-9